TWIG

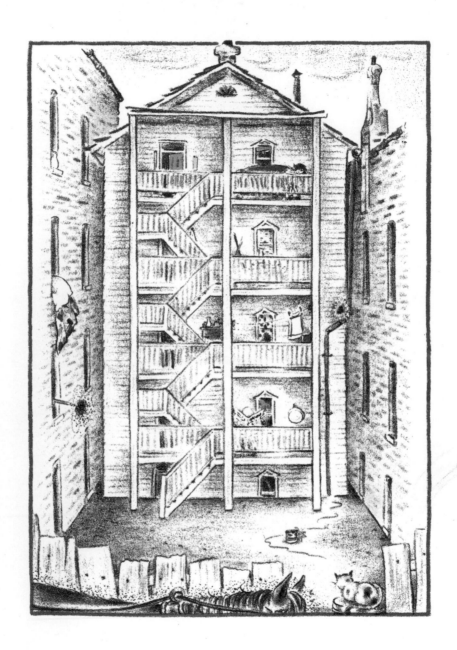

TWIG

60TH ANNIVERSARY EDITION

*

by

ELIZABETH ORTON JONES

KENTUCKY : PURPLE HOUSE PRESS : 2002

Published by
Purple House Press
PO Box 787, Cynthiana, KY 41031

Publisher's Cataloging in Publication Data
Jones, Elizabeth Orton.
TWIG / written and illustrated by Elizabeth Orton Jones
p. cm.
SUMMARY: Twig was a plain, ordinary little girl who found an empty tomato can
with pictures of bright red tomatoes all round it. When it was upside down, it looked
like a house just the right size for a fairy! This is the story of what happened in and
around that little house one Saturday afternoon.
ISBN: 1-930900-05-8
[1. Fantasy – Fiction 2. Magic – Fiction 3. Fairies – Fiction]   I. Title.
PZ7.J69 Tw 2001   Fic - dc21 00-111813

A Limited Edition of 200 books signed by the author is available from:
www.PurpleHousePress.com

Printed in China
4 5 6 7 8 9 10

TO LUCINDA

Dear Reader of this book,

whoever you are, wherever you may be — or

Dear Listener,

for somebody else might be reading this book to you — if so

Dear Somebody Else: —

Welcome to Twig's little world where, sooner or later, you will meet not only Twig but Elf, not only Old Boy the Horse and Old Girl the Cat, but Sparrow and Mrs. Sparrow and (sh! they're asleep now!) four squawky Sparrow children; and, later on in the story, not only Her Majesty the Fairy Queen but Lord Buzzle Cobb-Webb, a great magician who arrives from Fairyland on the Royal Magical Cobb-Webb Kerchief.

However, unless you get changed — as Twig did — from your usual size to a *very* small person, you will not be able to walk across the stick of gum bridge over the stream of drainpipe water, nor go in through the door of Twig's tomato can house, nor ride on Mrs. Sparrow's back up to her nest in the drainpipe's elbow, nor enjoy a comfortable ride in one of Old Horse's ears.

Elf will be too busy to change you, doing what he has to do in the story, even though he is gone much of the time — nobody knows where. Sparrow, too, is gone *most* of the time. But Elf always brings Twig a present when he comes home.

She doesn't always like what Elf brings, Chummie the Cockroach, for instance (you really must read about or listen to that!) . . . Anyway, I have my doubts about Elf being able to change you.

"What about Lord Buzzle, the great magician?" you might ask. "Couldn't *he* do it?" . . . Probably not, for he arrives too late in the story. I mean, you would miss a good many of the goings-on.

The Fairy Queen's arrival is rather late, too. But she *wouldn't* do it, I know. "Why not do it yourself?" she'd say. "Why not use what you already have: your own *i-ma-gi-na-tion?* It can do any kind of magic – anywhere – at any time. All you have to do is *use* it."

So – imagine yourself as a *very small* person – small enough to lie on a dandelion leaf with your arms hanging down – small enough to fly high in the air with a pair of butterfly wings attached to your back. Give it a try! If it works (and I bet it will) – why, then: have fun! . . . Afterwards, when the time comes to leave Twig's world and return to your own, you'll suddenly find yourself changed back, as Twig did when she heard her Mama call.

Then you'll begin to see things in *your* world that you never saw before; you'll have friends you never had before; and you'll understand what the Fairy Queen said to Twig as they sat side by side on a dandelion leaf, "Ends are also beginnings." and "Every single story has a beginning at its end."

With love and very best wishes –

Elizabeth Orton Jones
April, 2001

P.S. A message from Elf – by E(lf)Mail:

Iff yu happn 2 C tha Kweens furr wahndrin a rownd
sum whayr Hur Madjisty wood lyke 2 hav itt bak

e^l#f%] [f@a*i#r+y$l+a~n%d

CONTENTS

EXPECTING A FAIRY

IT WAS A SATURDAY MORNING in summer, and a little girl named Twig stood on the back porch which belonged to the fourth floor of a high sort of house in the city. That was where she lived, with her Mama and her Papa. Her Papa drove a yellow taxi.

Twig stood leaning against the porch's wooden railing, with her chin pressed down on the top of it. She had a piece of red ribbon from last Christmas tied on her hair, to keep it back. She had a piece of grocery string tied round and round one of her shoes, to keep it on. And she had a safety pin to fasten her dress, instead of buttons. She was looking down into the back yard. The back yard was her little world.

It was a square little world, bounded by houses on three of its sides and by a high fence on its other. Outside the fence was an alley. Inside, was a garbage can.

Out in the alley stood Old Boy, the ice-wagon horse, sound asleep as usual. He had worked all his life, poor Old Boy. He was very tired. He slept while he was standing up or while he was walking along. Also, he was very dusty. That made him sneeze.

PPPPPPPPPPPPPPPPPPPPPPPPPPPP! he would sneeze, out in the alley. Sneezing usually woke him up. But as soon as he woke up, he went to sleep again.

Old Boy, the ice-wagon horse, belonged to Twig's little world. But he wasn't much company.

On top of the garbage can sat Old Girl, the cat. She always sat there. She belonged to Twig's world, too. She had five or six colors of fur and five or six colors of whiskers. And she had a little motor inside of her. When she felt happy, she was supposed to turn her little motor on. When she didn't feel happy any more, she was supposed to turn it off. But most of the time she just left it running, for no reason at all, while she sat on the garbage can—the way Twig's Papa would leave the motor in his taxi running while he sat waiting for a fare.

Also, Old Girl could sing. She surely could! Almost every night she gave a concert. But during the day she just sat. Old Girl, the cat, wasn't much company either.

At the back of the house was a drainpipe. Halfway up, the drainpipe had an elbow. In the drainpipe's elbow was the Sparrows' nest. Twig had helped to build it. She had given the Sparrows several straws out of her Mama's broom, and a shoelace out of one of her Mama's shoes, and some pieces of grocery string, and part of an old, old spring out of the old, old sofa where her Papa took his snoozes on Saturday afternoons. Oh! Twig had given the Sparrows a good many things. The Sparrows belonged to her world, too.

Mrs. Sparrow was a busy little body who had her troubles. She had them with Sparrow. Sparrow was a gay bird. The nest was too quiet for him! He was gone most of the time. Poor little Mrs. Sparrow was always having to go after him and bring him home. But every time she brought him he went away again. The Sparrows weren't much company, either.

Down in the back yard no grass grew. But a dandelion stood there, all by itself. It had long leaves that were bent over like the branches of a tiny tree. And it had a tall stalk. At the top of its stalk was a little round bud—just a plain ordinary little round bud. But inside of it was a beautiful flower. Someday—maybe *today*—the little bud would open and let the flower show. Twig could see the dandelion from where she stood. It looked very green, away down there against the bare brown ground.

Along the ground, near the dandelion, ran a little stream of drainpipe water. The drainpipe had a leak. *Drip-drip-drip!* it went, most of the time. Twig had dug a little pathway, with a stick, for the drainpipe water to run in. That made a good little stream. Twig could see it now from where she stood. It looked no wider than a piece of grocery string, away down there on the ground.

Next to the dandelion, not far from the stream, stood an empty tomato can, upside down. Twig had found it yesterday, out in the alley. Somebody had thrown it away. There were pictures of bright red tomatoes all round it, and there was a place at the side of it where somebody's can opener had made a mistake. When it was upside down, it looked like a little house—with the can opener's mistake for its door. It looked just the right size for a fairy.

Twig had washed it clean with drainpipe water. She had stood it—just so!—upside down, next to the dandelion, not far from the stream. And there it had been ever since yesterday.

Twig hadn't told her Mama and her Papa, because they might think it was silly, but . . . ever since yesterday she had been expecting a fairy to come and live in the little house, and keep her company, and belong to her world. She had been expecting a pretty little fairy to come at any minute— all this time! But she hadn't seen a sign of one yet.

Well . . . maybe *today* a fairy would come!

"T-t-t-t-t-t!" said Mrs. Sparrow, sitting in her nest in the drainpipe's elbow, talking to herself. "Poor Twiggie! Poor little missy! Expecting a fairy! T-t-t-t-t!" Why! Mrs. Sparrow hadn't seen a fairy since she was a wee bird in the country. She had never even heard of a fairy in the city! She cocked her head—this way. Then she cocked her head— that way. After a while she cocked her head—this way again. "Well, well!" she said to herself at last. "I can't sit here all morning cocking my head! I'd better get busy!"

She hopped to the edge of the nest. She spread her wings. There was a *whirr-r-r-r!* and off she flew—over the back yard . . . over the garbage can . . . over the fence . . . and away over the city.

Twig watched her go.

Then . . .

Old Boy, the ice-wagon horse, sneezed — *PPPPPPPP-PPPPPPPP!* — out in the alley.

13

Old Girl, the cat, stood up on top of the garbage can, turned round, and sat down again.

A voice called, "Twig! Come and help me with the dishes, will you, please?"

That was her Mama's voice. So Twig took her chin from the railing and ran into the house.

★

ELF

M RS. SPARROW HAD BEEN LOOKING for Sparrow all
morning. She had been looking for him everywhere.
She had been flying hither and thither, up one street and
down another, past buildings and houses and pretty green
parks. But Sparrow was nowhere to be seen.

"T-t-t-t-t!" said Mrs. Sparrow, talking to herself as she
flew. "I wonder where he can be *this* time!"

She flew near to the front of a huge building. It was the
Public Library. She looked about once more for Sparrow.
But Sparrow was not there. "Well, I think I'll just drop
down and sit a bit, before I start home," she said to herself.

So down she dropped, and sat on a corner of the top
library step. People were coming and going, up and down.
Mrs. Sparrow sat there resting her wings and watching the
people's feet. She saw all kinds: young feet—old feet—big
feet—very big feet. And then she saw something . . . quite
surprising!

She saw a little fellow, not much taller than she, come out of one of the huge library doors. She saw him come out and begin to jump up and down on the top step, right among the people's feet. His cap was on the very back of his head, and under one arm he had a bright red book about the size of a two-cent stamp.

"Well, I never in all my life!" said Mrs. Sparrow, hopping over to him. "Come here, little fellow, before you're stepped on!" She guided him safely to the corner, with her wing.

There he began to jump up and down some more. He seemed very much excited.

"Why are you so excited, little fellow?" asked Mrs. Sparrow.

"Hm?" he squeaked.

"I say—why are you so excited?"

"I'm going!" he squeaked, jumping up and down.

"Well, well!" chirped Mrs. Sparrow. "Going where?"

He stood still. He lifted his shoulders several times. "I don't know!" he squeaked.

"You don't know!" Mrs. Sparrow began to chuckle. She just couldn't help it. She chuckled till her feathers shook. Then she said, "Tell me your name, little fellow!"

So he told her. His name was Elf.

Everything he had on matched, and was brown and

crinkly like leather. Mrs. Sparrow reached over and pinched the edge of his jacket a little, with her bill. "Well, well!" she said. "What kind of skin?"

"Hm?"

"I say—what kind of skin are your clothes all made of?"

"Potato," squeaked Elf, looking down at them. "Why?"

"I just wondered—" Mrs. Sparrow chuckled some more. Then she cocked her head—this way—and looked Elf over. She cocked her head—that way—and looked him over again. "Just the right size!" she kept saying to herself. "Just the

17

right size!" At last she said to him, "Little fellow, how would you like to hop on my back and come along with me?"

"I'd like to very much!" squeaked Elf.

"Hop on, then!" said Mrs. Sparrow.

So Elf hopped on Mrs. Sparrow's back and sat astride, with his legs beneath her wings. He held tight to her feathers with one hand, and with the other he held tight to his book.

"Up we go!" chirped Mrs. Sparrow, spreading her wings.

And up they went.

Soon roofs and chimneys and streets and parks were all spread out below them. There were signs on the roofs, there was smoke puffing out of the chimneys, there were all sorts of things moving up and down the streets, and there was green grass growing in the parks. Elf had never seen such a grand sight. He turned this way and that, on Mrs. Sparrow's back.

"Sit still, if you please, little fellow!" said Mrs. Sparrow as she flew.

So Elf sat still, whistling a careless little tune—over and over, the way fellows do.

"Where in the world are we going?" he squeaked, after they had been flying along for quite a while.

"To the back yard behind the house where Twig lives," explained Mrs. Sparrow.

"Who's Twig?" squeaked Elf.

"Twig's a little girl," explained Mrs. Sparrow. "Well . . . she's quite a *big* girl, compared with you! But not too big. We like her, Sparrow and I."

"Where do you and Sparrow live?" squeaked Elf.

"In a nest!" chirped Mrs. Sparrow, without mentioning any of her little troubles.

"Is there room in your nest for me?" squeaked Elf.

"Plenty of room, little fellow!" said Mrs. Sparrow, chuckling as she flew. "But I'm afraid our nest is rather high up for you. Down below, though, is a pretty little house, just your size!"

Suddenly Mrs. Sparrow darted up an alley. Quick as a wink she turned and sailed over a fence into a back yard. She circled down, skimmed along the ground, and made her landing.

"Well, here . . . we . . . are!" she said, rather out of breath.

And, sure enough, there stood a little house, just Elf's size, with bright red pictures all round it. Beside it stood a green tree, just Elf's size too, with lovely long green branches. And there, close by, ran a little stream of water—Elf's size. Why, Elf had never seen anything like it!

Quickly he slipped from Mrs. Sparrow's back. He ran to the doorway of the little house and peeked in. "Hoo hoo!" he squeaked. "Does anybody live here?"

No answer.

"Does anybody live here—I say!"

No answer.

"Yippee!" squeaked Elf, jumping up and down. *"I do, then!"* And, thanking Mrs. Sparrow for the ride, he took off his cap and walked in.

"I *thought* you'd like it, little fellow!" chuckled Mrs. Sparrow. She hopped to the stream and took a drink of drainpipe water. She chuckled again. Then she spread her wings and flew up to the nest, to see if Sparrow had come home yet.

★

DOWN THE STEPS

IT WAS SATURDAY AFTERNOON, and a woman in a big blue dress was sweeping the porch which belonged to the fourth floor, at the back of the house, where Twig lived. That was Twig's Mama. She was sweeping around and around the old, old sofa. Out of the bottom of the old, old sofa hung several of its old, old springs. On top of the old, old sofa Twig's Papa lay, taking a snooze, with his handkerchief over his face.

"*Honk . . . whee!*" snored Twig's Papa. "*Honk . . . wheeee-ee-ee!*"

Every time he snored, his handkerchief flew up from his face and floated gently down again. Every time he snored, the old, old springs of the old, old sofa—rattled.

Twig was going down the steps to the back yard. They were zigzag steps and there were a good many of them. Halfway down the first flight of steps she stopped and called to her Mama, "Did you say something, Mama?"

21

"*Sh!*" whispered Twig's Mama, shaking the broom over the railing. "Don't disturb your Papa! I only said it's a hot day—hotter than yesterday, even!"

Yes, it was hot. But Twig didn't mind. She waved good-bye to her Mama and went skipping down the steps. She had several things in her pocket. They rattled when she skipped.

At the bottom of the first flight of steps was another back porch, just like the higher one except that it was lower. It belonged to the third floor and on it were a broom, a mop, a big broken box, and a clothesbasket. Twig tiptoed to the clothesbasket and peeked in.

"Dear!" she whispered, very, very softly so as not to wake Mrs. Webb's little baldheaded baby. For there he lay, inside the basket, sound asleep.

Webb was a traveling salesman. Like Sparrow, he was gone most of the time. He sold Royal Magical Vacuum Cleaners.

Whooooooooooooo — whoooooooooo — oooooo — ooo! went Mrs. Webb's Royal Magical Vacuum Cleaner, inside the house.

Twig leaned away down close and smiled at Mrs. Webb's little baldheaded baby. *"Dear!"* she whispered, very, very softly, again. Then she went tiptoeing down the next flight of steps.

At the bottom of the next flight of steps was another back porch. It belonged to the second floor, and there stood Blondie Buzzle hanging up some wash. Blondie was a grown-up girl—oh! a lady, really. She surely was beautiful! Her eyes were blue, and her hair was as yellow as Twig's Papa's taxi.

Twig looked and looked at Blondie.

"Hello, Twig!" said Blondie, with a clothespin in her mouth.

"Hel-lo!" said Twig, smiling very sweetly because Blondie was so beautiful.

23

Squa-a-a-a-w-w-w-k! Squa-a-a-a-w-w-w-k! went Mrs. Buzzle's radio, inside the house. Somebody shouted: "Make your old coat new—by magic!—with a smart fox fur!" "HELLO THERE, SWEETIE PIE!" shrieked somebody else. Then Mrs. Buzzle's radio went *Squa-a-a-a-w-w-w-k!* again, and was still.

Twig looked some more at Blondie. Then she waved good-bye and went skipping down the *next* flight of steps.

At the bottom of the *next* flight of steps was *another* back porch. It belonged to the first floor, and there sat old Mr. Cobb, the landlord, reading the newspaper, as usual.

"How-do, Mr. Cobb, sir!" said Twig. "How's the world?" She didn't really want to know how it was. But everybody

24

tried to be as polite as possible to old Mr. Cobb, because he was the landlord. And that was the question Twig's Papa always asked.

"Well . . ." began Mr. Cobb, behind his newspaper, as usual.

And, as usual, Twig had to wait for him to think of a word that was big enough to take in the whole world at once. She waited . . . and waited . . . and waited . . . and waited. She slipped her hand into her pocket and felt the things that were there. She looked down at her feet. She turned her toes in. Then she turned them out. Then she turned them in and out, in and out, fast, like a little dance.

25

The little dance took her closer—closer to the railing of Mr. Cobb's porch, until she was looking over it into the back yard. My, but the back yard was *near* now!

It was so near that Twig could see the very tomatoes in the pictures all round the little house. It was so near that she could hear the very *drip-drip-drip* of the water from the drainpipe's leak. It was so near that she could hear something else! Something . . . quite surprising! It sounded like somebody whistling a careless little tune!

Was somebody there? . . . Was it a fairy? . . . Was it the pretty little fairy that Twig had been expecting ever since yesterday?

She didn't wait any longer for Mr. Cobb to think of his word. She ran down the last flight of steps, two at a time to the ground. Then she went tiptoeing to the little house. She looked all around. But she didn't see a sign of a fairy. She listened. But she didn't even hear the whistling any more.

Maybe the pretty little fairy was hiding!

Twig leaned away down close to the little house. "Hoo hoo!" she called, very, very softly. "You don't need to be afraid!"

Afraid! . . . Out through the doorway marched a little tiny fellow with his arms folded grandly in front of him and his knees going wobble-wobble. Afraid!

Twig had to hold both her hands over her mouth for a minute to keep from laughing. Then she sat down on the ground and doubled up her legs and said, "Well?"

The little tiny fellow just stood there with his arms folded and his knees going wobble-wobble. . . . Well, what?

"Well, for goodness sakes!" said Twig. "Who are *you?*"

"I'm Elf!" said Elf.

And his voice sounded like the little tiny squeak which was in Twig's Papa's Sunday shoes.

MAGIC

"ARE YOU INTERESTED IN MAGIC?" squeaked Elf. He was sitting, cross-legged, on the ground near the dandelion, with his little red book open on his lap.

"Oh, I don't know," said Twig, taking the things out of her pocket. "Why? Are you?"

"I'll say I am!" squeaked Elf. "I'll *say* I am!" And his whole little tiny face shone with saying that he was.

Twig reached over and put an old thimble of her Mama's very carefully, with two fingers, into the little house. Next she put in a bottletop. Then she stood an old feather of Mrs. Sparrow's beside the door. She had brought these things for the pretty little fairy to keep house with. The thimble was a cooking pot; the bottletop was a table; and Mrs. Sparrow's feather was a broom, to sweep the floor.

"See this book?" squeaked Elf. "It's all about magic!"

"Is that so?" said Twig, taking a stick of gum out of her pocket. "Do *you* know how to do magic?"

"It tells how in the book," squeaked Elf. "All *I* have to know is how to read!"

"Can you read?" asked Twig, unwrapping the piece of shiny paper from the stick of gum.

"Didn't you just *see* me reading?"

"Mm-hmm," said Twig.

"Well, then!" squeaked Elf grandly. And he went back to his book.

Twig smoothed out the piece of shiny paper and laid it on the ground. She was about to take a bite of the stick of gum when she had an idea. Reaching over, she laid it—just so!—across the stream of drainpipe water. It made a good little bridge. Twig had never seen such a good little bridge!

"Elf!" she said. "Look!"

"I'm busy!" squeaked Elf. He turned to the back of his book and began to run his finger down the page—the way Twig's Mama always did when she was looking up what to cook, in the cook book.

"What are you looking up?" asked Twig.

"I'm looking up what kind of magic to do!" squeaked Elf.

"Why don't you do the kind where you change yourself into something else?" said Twig. "You know — the way magicians do in stories?"

"All right!" squeaked Elf. "What'll I be?"

Twig thought and thought. "How about being a pretty little fairy?" she asked after a while.

"No!" squeaked Elf.

"Wouldn't you like to be a pretty little fairy?" said Twig. "*I* would!"

"Well, then!" squeaked Elf grandly. "I'll change *you!*"

"Me!" said Twig. Now she was *very much* interested. "Really? Could you change—*me*—into a pretty little fairy?"

"Sure!" squeaked Elf. "Why not?"

"Well, I'm rather big," said Twig.

"The bigger the better!" squeaked Elf, running his finger partway down the page. Suddenly he slapped the book shut and opened it again, to page thirty-seven.

"Does it look hard?" asked Twig.

Whistling his careless little tune, Elf turned the book around for Twig to see. And this is how it looked:

```
sodasoda- -
sarsaparilla
sodasoda- -
sarsaparilla
sodasoda- -
sarsaparilla
37
```

"Very easy—very easy," squeaked Elf, turning the book around again. "All right!"

30

"Is it . . . going to . . . hurt?" asked Twig.

"Of course not!" squeaked Elf. "It's *magic!* Shut your eyes!"

So Twig shut her eyes. After a while she said, "Elf . . . what in the world are you doing?"

"I'm doing the magic!" squeaked Elf. "Keep quiet!"

So Twig kept quiet. Then, after a while, she said, "Elf . . . what if you made a mistake?"

"Hm?"

"I say—what if you made a *mistake?*"

"Oh, you might get changed into something else—that's all," squeaked Elf. "A cockroach or something."

"A *cockroach!*" said Twig. "Say! Will you please try *not* to make a mistake?"

"Will you please try to keep *quiet!*" squeaked Elf.

So Twig kept quiet.

And finally, after a long time, she heard Elf slap the book shut. She heard Elf say, "All right! Open your eyes!"

Slowly Twig opened her eyes. . . . Why, the whole back yard looked different! . . . She jumped up. . . . Why, she wasn't even as high as the dandelion! . . . Why, she was no taller than Elf! She was *tiny!*

Elf was on the other side of the stream. Twig smiled across at him sweetly. She stood on tiptoe. She took a little step on tiptoe. She waved her arms, very, very gracefully. Then she began to dance. Oh! Wasn't it lovely being a fairy? Wasn't it lovely, having *wings?*" She wiggled her shoulders. But she didn't seem to *feel* any wings!

"Elf!" she said, stopping still as a statue. "I *am* a fairy—aren't I?"

Without waiting for an answer she ran to the piece of shiny paper that lay on the ground, and leaned over it to see.

But what she saw was no different from what she usually saw when she looked into a mirror. It was—just Twig . . . with the same old dress on . . . just Twig, with the same old hair . . . just Twig, the same all over, except that she was tiny.

Oh-oh!

She scuffed one shoe against the ground a few times. Then she walked to the stick-of-gum bridge, and across it to the other side. She walked right past Elf without saying a word. She walked straight to the little house, took Mrs. Sparrow's feather from its place by the door, went in, and began sweeping the floor *just as hard as she could!*

Out rolled the thimble. Out flew the bottletop. Clouds of dust came floating out. Elf crawled quickly underneath the dandelion, to be out of the way.

At last the dust died down, and Twig came out. She stood Mrs. Sparrow's feather in its place by the door. She skipped to the dandelion, crawled underneath, and sat down beside Elf.

And after a while she said, "Elf?"

And he said, "Hm?"

And she said, "It's only that . . . it's only that . . . it's only that . . ." She took a deep breath. "Well, anyway, I'm not a cockroach!" she said.

★

33

MRS. SPARROW'S NEST

TWIG WAS GETTING the little house all settled, in case somebody should come to call.

"Elf," she said, "run and bring our cooking pot, will you, please?"

So Elf ran and brought back Twig's Mama's thimble, carrying it in his arms.

"Now, Elf," said Twig, "run and bring our mirror, will you, please?"

So Elf ran and brought back the piece of shiny paper, dragging it behind him.

"Now, Elf," said Twig, "run and bring our table, will you, please?"

So Elf ran and brought back the bottletop, rolling it on its edge along the ground. By this time he wanted to sit down on something good and comfortable, with his book!

"And *now*, Elf—" said Twig.

Elf was just beginning to wonder how long this sort of thing could go on when they heard a *whirr-r-r!* and there stood Mrs. Sparrow.

"Oh! Mrs. Sparrow! Hello!" squeaked Elf. He was *very* glad she had come.

"Hello there, little fellow!" said Mrs. Sparrow. "How are you getting along? . . . Why, bless my feathers! Who's *this?*"

Elf took a deep breath and looked very tired. "It's Twig," he said.

Twig! Mrs. Sparrow could hardly believe it. She cocked her head—this way. Then she cocked her head—that way. After a while she cocked her head—this way again. "Well, well, little missy!" she said at last. "You surely have shrunk! How did you ever do it?"

"Elf did it. By magic," explained Twig.

"Magic!" said Mrs. Sparrow. "Well, I declare! What next?" She looked at the table, the cooking pot, the mirror,

35

and her own old feather in its place by the door. "I see you're keeping house, little missy!" she said.

"Elf's helping me," said Twig. "We've got everything all settled—almost!"

"*Almost!*" said Elf, sitting down on the ground. "Whew!" But Twig made him get right up again, because it wasn't polite for him to sit down while Mrs. Sparrow was standing.

"Ask *her* to sit down!" whispered Twig.

So Elf asked her.

"Thank you, little fellow," replied Mrs. Sparrow, "but I'd rather stand up for a change, if you don't mind. I've been sitting on my eggs for the last hour!"

"Eggs!" squeaked Twig, very much interested. "Why, Mrs. Sparrow! How many eggs have you?"

"Four, little missy," said Mrs. Sparrow proudly, "and

they're perfect beauties! . . . At least," she added, "that's what *I* think!"

"What does Sparrow think—*ouch!*" said Elf. Twig had just poked him, because it wasn't polite to bring up people's little troubles right in front of them. Why, Sparrow probably hadn't even seen Mrs. Sparrow's eggs!

Twig stepped close to Mrs. Sparrow and put an arm round her, as far as it would go. "I wish *I* could see your eggs, Mrs. Sparrow!" she said, smiling very sweetly.

Mrs. Sparrow chuckled. "All right, little missy!" she said. "Hop on!"

Twig was on Mrs. Sparrow's back in no time. "Hop on, too, Elf!" she squeaked.

So Elf hopped on, too, behind Twig.

"Up we go!" chirped Mrs. Sparrow, spreading her wings.

"Oh! Wait a minute, please, Mrs. Sparrow!" said Elf. "I almost forgot something!"

So Mrs. Sparrow waited while Elf hopped off and hopped on again, this time with his book.

"Honestly, Elf!" said Twig. "What do you want a book for?"

"To read, of course!" said Elf.

Again Mrs. Sparrow spread her wings. "Up we go!" she chirped.

And up they went, so fast that Twig had time only to squeak, "Oh, Elf! . . . Hold on! . . . *Elf!*"—before they were there.

"I'm afraid *my* house isn't very tidy today," said Mrs. Sparrow, lighting on the edge of the nest.

No, it surely wasn't. There were pieces of grocery string, and straws from Twig's Mama's broom, and hairs from Old Boy's long, long tail, and some safety pins, and *many* old feathers, and a piece of silver tinsel from a last year's Christmas tree, and one of Twig's Mama's shoelaces, and a pink corset string, and a toothpick, and a hook and eye and some buttons, and some picture wire, and a carpet tack with some carpet stuck to it, and a little faded American flag from the Fourth of July, and a rusty hairpin, and part of an old, old spring out of the old, old sofa where Twig's Papa took his snoozes on Saturday afternoons—and a burnt match, and the first six inches of a tape measure, and another rusty hairpin, and a little torn piece of paper. *"Sweetheart,"* it said in purple ink, and some bright pink pearls strung together, and a stick from an all-day sucker, and a little limp piece of rubber from an old green balloon— Oh! Twig had never seen such a mess!

But right there in the bottom were four perfectly beautiful eggs with little tiny freckles on top of them, like pepper.

"Slide in, little fellow—little missy," chirped Mrs. Sparrow, sitting on the edge of the nest. "Just make yourselves at home!"

39

So Twig and Elf hopped down from Mrs. Sparrow's back and slid in.

Twig stepped to one of the eggs and leaned away down close and patted it. *"Dear!"* she whispered, very, very softly, to the egg. Then she stepped to another egg and leaned away down close and patted *it*. *"Dear!"* she whispered, very, very softly, again. Then she whispered, "Mrs. Sparrow, could I—could I—could I sit on one of your eggs?"

"Could *I* sit on another?" whispered Elf.

Mrs. Sparrow nodded her head. Of course they could, if they were careful.

So Twig sat down, very carefully, on one egg. Elf, very carefully, sat down on another and crossed his legs and opened his book—*at last!*

Twig and Mrs. Sparrow winked at each other. "Nothing like having a good comfortable egg to sit down on, is there, little fellow?" said Mrs. Sparrow.

"Hm?" asked Elf.

But Mrs. Sparrow couldn't answer for chuckling. She chuckled till the whole nest shook.

A QUIET LITTLE TIME

A S SOON AS THEY were down again from Mrs. Sparrow's
nest, Twig said, "Now, Elf—"

But before she could finish what she was going to say,
Elf had put on his cap and was walking away, in the direction of the garbage can, with his little red book.

"What are you going away for?" called Twig after him.

But Elf didn't answer. He just kept walking.

"Well, did you ever!" said Twig, standing in the doorway with her hands on her hips, watching Elf grow smaller
and smaller as he walked farther and farther away.

She took a deep breath. Then she lifted the thimble and
carried it into the house and set it in place—just so!—in the
middle. She rolled the bottletop in on its edge and lifted
it up and laid it—just so!—on the thimble. Sure enough, that
made a good little table. Twig had never seen such a good
little table! Next she dragged the piece of shiny paper in
through the door and smoothed it out—just so!—against the
wall. Then she dusted off her hands, one against the other.

There! Everything was settled! Now she could go out and sit underneath the dandelion and have a quiet little time, all by herself, till Elf came home.

So she went out. But instead of sitting underneath the dandelion she climbed up onto one of its long green leaves and lay there, with her cheek against the leaf and her arms

hanging over. The leaf moved up and down with her. She gave a little push against the ground with one hand. The leaf moved up and down again. She gave another little push. The leaf moved up and down *again.* She kept making it move up and down by giving little pushes against the ground, first with one hand and then with the other.

Oh! Wasn't this lovely? Wasn't it lovely being little enough to lie on a dandelion leaf?

She made the leaf move up and down once more. Then she turned over and lay on her back, with her arms folded behind her head. She looked up at the leaves above her. Here and there between the leaves she could see little pieces of sky, all different shapes, showing through. One little piece of sky was shaped like a shirt. Another was shaped like a hat. Here was one shaped like a long, pointed shoe. And there was one without much shape, like the old, old sofa where Twig's Papa took his snoozes on Saturday afternoons.

Oh! Wasn't *this* lovely? Wasn't it lovely being down low enough to have leaves between you and the sky?

Twig found one more little piece of sky, shaped like a ship. Then she closed her eyes and lay still. My, but it was quiet! It was so quiet that Twig could hear the drainpipe water running along in the stream. It sounded as if it were whispering: *Sodasodasarsaparilla! Sodasodasarsaparilla! Sodasodasarsaparilla! Sodasodasarsaparilla!*

Oh! Wasn't *this* lovely? Wasn't it lovely being quiet enough to hear what the water in a little stream is whispering as it runs along?

But suddenly it wasn't quiet any more, for just at that moment Elf came running home. He came running for dear

life—dashing past the dandelion—diving through the doorway into the little house. Then there was

    1. A bump

    2. An *ouch!*

    3. A clatter. . . .

And Twig jumped from the leaf.

"Well, for goodness sakes!" she said, standing in the
doorway with her hands on her hips.

Elf was sitting in the middle of the floor, with one leg in
the thimble, hugging the bottletop tight with both arms.
His cap was over one ear. His book, fallen open, lay at
Twig's feet. She picked it up and dusted it off.

"What *is* the matter?" she asked.

"Whew!" said Elf, with his breath going in and out, in and out, fast. "I . . . I . . . I—"

"You what?" asked Twig.

"I . . . *saw*—" said Elf.

"Saw what?" asked Twig.

"Saw . . . *two*—" said Elf.

"Two what?" asked Twig.

"Two . . . *whew!*" said Elf.

"Is that so?" said Twig. "Now, Elf—get up and help me put the table together, will you, please?"

"Listen!" said Elf, getting up and tiptoeing to the doorway with his knees going wobble-wobble. "Didn't you just hear me telling you what I saw? This is no time for putting tables together!" He peeked out. "Whew!" he whispered. "Look at that one!"

"What one?" asked Twig. "Where?"

Elf pointed in the direction of the garbage can. "See— right there on top?" he whispered. "And the other one's out in the alley. The other one's *much bigger,* even!"

Twig looked in the direction of the garbage can. Then she looked at Elf. After a while she looked in the direction of the garbage can again. After another while she looked back at Elf. She had to hold both her hands over her mouth

45

for a minute to keep from laughing. Then she took her hands away. "Honestly, Elf! Didn't . . . you . . . ever . . . see . . . a . . . plain . . . ordinary . . . cat . . . before?" she asked, very slowly and patiently.

Elf made a foolish face and shook his head.

"Or . . . a . . . plain . . . ordinary . . . ice-wagon horse . . . either?"

Elf made another foolish face and shook his head again.

Well, where . . . in . . . the . . . world . . . have . . . you . . . been . . . that . . . you . . . never . . . saw . . . a . . . plain . . . ordinary . . . cat . . . or . . . a . . . plain . . . ordinary . . . ice-wagon horse?" asked Twig, very slowly and patiently.

"I've been in a story," said Elf.

"In a—*story!*" said Twig, with her eyes nearly popping out of her head. "Why, Elf!" she whispered. "Were you —*really*—in a story?"

"Sure!" said Elf.

"What *kind* of story?" whispered Twig.

Elf took a deep breath and folded his arms in front of him. "Just . . . a . . . plain . . . ordinary . . . story," he said, very slowly and patiently. Then he began to whistle his careless little tune.

★

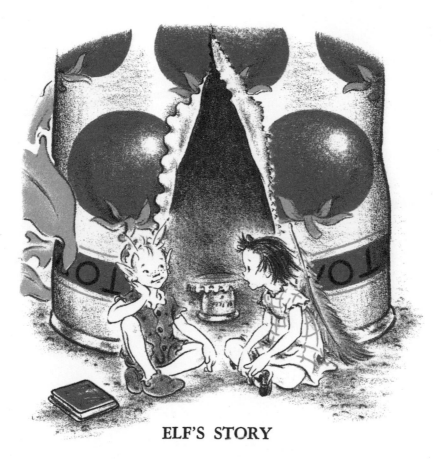

ELF'S STORY

WHAT DOES IT FEEL LIKE, being in a story?" asked Twig, sitting down in the doorway.

"It feels the same as this," said Elf, sitting down beside her. "No different."

"Well, tell about it!" said Twig. "What did you do in the story?"

"Sat on a sack of potatoes," said Elf, "down in Old Shoemaker's cellar."

"O-o-o-oh!" said Twig, nodding her head up and down. "Did Old Shoemaker make your clothes?"

"Sure!" said Elf, looking down at them. "Why?"

But Twig didn't stop to say why. "Was Old Shoemaker so poor that he only had enough leather to make one pair of shoes?" she asked.

"He was much poorer than that," said Elf. "He was so poor he didn't have any leather."

"Well, what did *you* make the shoes out of in the middle of the night?" asked Twig.

"Me! Make the shoes! In the middle of the night!" said Elf. "What are you talking about?"

"I'm talking about what happened in the story," said Twig. "Isn't that what happened?"

"No!" said Elf.

"What *did* happen, then?" asked Twig.

"Well . . ." said Elf, crossing his legs and folding his arms in front of him. Then he began to tell the story, by heart. . . .

Old Shoemaker was very poor. He had nothing in the world but a little old house, a medium-sized old Wife, and a big old sack of potatoes down in his cellar. He had no money with which to buy leather. He had no leather with which to make shoes. So he had nothing to do but sit in his Wife's kitchen.

Now one evening Old Shoemaker's Wife went down the steps to the cellar, to get some potatoes out of the sack to make some soup for Old Shoemaker's supper. And just as she leaned over the sack, to take the potatoes out, she saw something . . . quite surprising! She saw a little tiny fellow, all dressed in potato skins, sitting on the sack. . . .

"That was *me!*" explained Elf proudly.

"Yes, I know," said Twig. "Go on!"

" '. . . little tiny fellow . . . sitting on the sack,' " mumbled Elf to himself. Then he went on:

The little tiny fellow said, "Please, ma'am, if you'll not take any of these potatoes, I'll grant you a wish— anything you like, ma'am!"

"Why, Elf!" said Twig. "Can *you* grant wishes?"

"Of course not!" said Elf. "Not *really.* That was just my part in the story."

"O-o-o-oh!" said Twig, nodding her head up and down. "I see! It's like being in a play! Once I was in a play. My Mama and my Papa came and how my Papa clapped! I was a fairy, and *this* is what *I* was supposed to say." . . . Twig jumped up and waved her arms, very, very gracefully, while she said, " 'Fairies all, come dance tonight—every elf . . . and . . . every sprite!' " Then she began to dance.

"Say! Whose story is this?" said Elf. "I was just going to tell what happened!"

"All right!" said Twig, sitting down again in the doorway. "What did?"

" ' ". . . a wish—anything you like, ma'am!" ' " mumbled Elf to himself. Then he went on:

"Mercy gracious me!" said Old Shoemaker's Wife.

And Twig burst out laughing, because Elf sounded *just like* Old Shoemaker's Wife. "Well, go on!" she said when she had laughed enough.

Elf mumbled, " '. . . said Old Shoemaker's Wife.' " He went on:

Then she turned around and ran right up the steps, three at a time—

"Three at a time!" said Twig. "How could an old woman run up the steps three at a time?"

Elf took a deep breath. "Say!" he said. "If you don't keep quiet you'll never hear the end of this story!"

" '. . . steps, three at a time,' " he mumbled; then he went on:

. . . to tell Old Shoemaker about her wish.

"What would you wish for if I were you?" asked Old Shoemaker's Wife when she told him.

"Why, a piece of leather, of course!" said Old Shoemaker.

And Twig burst out laughing again, because Elf sounded *just like* Old Shoemaker. "Well, go on!" she said when she had laughed enough.

Elf took another deep breath. "'. . . said Old Shoe-maker," he mumbled. Then he went on once more:

"A piece of leather!" said Old Shoemaker's Wife. "What would *I* do with a piece of smelly old leather? I'd rather have a fine silk dress, gathered at the waist-line, with tiny woolen tassels all round the hem!"

And Old Shoemaker said, "I was only telling you what *I'd* wish for! Smelly old leather indeed! Brand-new leather is what it would be! A brand-new pair of shoes is what I would make! And I'd sell them for enough money to buy *another* piece of leather!"

"Another piece of leather!" said Old Shoemaker's Wife. And when, pray, would I have my fine silk dress, gathered at the waistline, with tiny woolen tas-sels all round the hem?"

"When I had enough money to pay for it, of course!" said Old Shoemaker.

"And why not wish for money in the first place?" said his Wife.

And Old Shoemaker said, "Now look here! I'm an honest man! What money I get, I work for!"

"Yes, and at *your* rate of work," said his Wife, "I'd have a fine silk dress, gathered at the waistline, with tiny woolen tassels all round the hem—to be *buried* in!"

"I'll thank you to hold your tongue!" said Old Shoemaker.

"I'll thank *you* to hold *yours!*" said his Wife. And then she began to cry. "Oh, my! Oh, my!" she cried. "I wish this story would begin all over again! It's getting worse and worse!"

"Well for goodness sakes!" said Twig. "Is that the end?"

"Sure!" said Elf.

"Did she get her wish?" asked Twig.

"Of course!" said Elf.

"And where were *you* while all that was going on?"

"Sitting on the sack of potatoes," said Elf, "down in the cellar, waiting for the story to begin again."

Twig was quiet for a minute. Then she said, "I don't think you had a very good part in that story! I'm glad you're out of it."

"I'm glad, too!" said Elf.

"But," said Twig, sitting up straight, "what I'd like to know is: how did you *get* out of it?"

"How did I . . . him?" said Elf, with his face suddenly turning as red as the tomatoes in the pictures all round the little house. "Oh, that! . . . *That!* . . . Why, that . . . er . . . that . . . well, that's *another* story!"

★

53

CHUMMIE

ELF WAS GONE. He had been gone a number of times. But each time he had come back. And each time he had brought something back with him, for Twig.

One time he had brought back an old toothpaste top. It made a good little dish. Twig had never seen such a good little dish! She had set it—just so!—in the middle of the table. Then she had said, "Thanks, Elf!"

The next time, Elf had brought back another old toothpaste top. It made another good little dish. Twig had set it—just so!—beside the first, on the table. Then she had said, "Thanks, Elf!"

The *next* time, Elf had brought back *another* old toothpaste top. It made *another* good little dish. Twig had set it —just so!—beside the other two, on the table. Then she had said, "Thanks, Elf!"

Now she wondered what Elf was going to bring back *this* time. She was sitting in the doorway watching for him. She watched and watched.

And finally, after a long time, she heard him whistling his careless little tune, away off. As he came nearer, his little tune grew louder. And pretty soon Twig saw him. She saw that he was *not* bringing another old toothpaste top. She saw that he was bringing quite a big thing this time. He was dragging it behind him. No, he wasn't either! It seemed to be coming all by itself. But how *could* anything come all by itself? What was it? Twig looked and looked. And pretty soon she saw that the thing had legs. Yes, it had. It had six legs. She could count them. Then she saw that the thing had two long feelers, waving in the air. And *then*, all of a sudden, she knew. She *knew* it was a cockroach!

Oh-oh!

She jumped up, ran to the dandelion, and climbed onto its highest leaf.

"Hoo hoo!" called Elf as he came near.

Behind him came the cockroach.

"Hoo hoo!" called Elf again. "Hoo hoo! Twig! Where are you? . . . Oh, there you are! What are you sitting up there for?"

"Never mind why!" said Twig from her leaf.

"Look what I brought *this* time!" said Elf proudly.

"I *am* looking," said Twig.

"His name is Chummie!" said Elf. "Isn't he *cute?*"

"Cute!" said Twig.

"What's the matter? Don't you like him?" asked Elf.

"Like him!" said Twig. "I hate him!"

"*I* like him!" said Elf. And he sat down on the ground, took Chummie in his arms and hugged him.

"Honestly, Elf!" said Twig from her leaf. "Before I'd hug a cockroach!"

Elf set Chummie down. "Roll over!" he said. "Over!" And Chummie rolled over. "Isn't *that* cute?" said Elf proudly. "*I* taught him that!"

"Well, well!" said Twig from her leaf.

"I'm going to teach him lots of things!" said Elf.

"I hope you're not going to teach him to come into my house!" said Twig.

Elf jumped up. "Come on, Chummie!" he said, walking toward the house. "Here, Chummie-Chummie!"

And Chummie followed.

"See?" said Elf. "He goes every place I go!"

Elf went into the house. And Chummie followed.

Twig slid down from her leaf. She ran to the doorway. "Elf!" she said. "You get that cockroach out of here this minute, or I'll—"

"Hm?" asked Elf, skipping round and round, inside the house, with Chummie scooting round and round after him.

Twig ran to the table and picked up two of the toothpaste tops, one in each hand. She waited for Chummie to come

scooting round again. She waited until he was right near
the doorway. Then she threw both the toothpaste tops at

him, one after the other. "Take that!" she screamed. "And
that!" she screamed. And now—get *out!*"

Chummie scooted out quickly. Elf scooted out quickly,
too.

Away scooted Chummie. And away walked Elf.

"Elf!" called Twig from the doorway. "I didn't mean
you!"

But Elf paid no attention. He kept right on walking, in
the direction of the garbage can, with Chummie scooting
on ahead.

"You're not *mad,* are you, Elf?" called Twig.

Elf didn't even turn his head. He kept right on walking.

"Are you, Elf?" called Twig.

Farther and farther away walked Elf.

Twig stood watching until Chummie and Elf had both
turned round the end of the fence and were out of sight.
Then she began to cry. She cried and she cried and she cried.
And finally, after a long time, she stopped crying. She even
laughed a little, because she had sounded so much like Old

Shoemaker's Wife. She took a deep breath. Then she picked up the two toothpaste tops and set them—just so!—

on the table. Next she took Mrs. Sparrow's feather from its place and did a little sweeping around where Chummie had been. She stood Mrs. Sparrow's feather in its place again and dusted off her hands, one against the other. Then she sat down in the doorway.

"Now!" she said. "Let's begin this all over again!"

★

ALL OVER AGAIN

ELF WAS GONE. He had been gone a number of times. But each time he had come back. And each time he had brought something back with him, for Twig.

One time he had brought back an old toothpaste top. It made a good little dish. Twig had never seen such a good little dish! She had set it—just so!—in the middle of the table. Then she had said, "Thanks, Elf!"

The next time, Elf had brought back another old toothpaste top. It made another good little dish. Twig had set it —just so!—beside the first, on the table. Then she had said, "Thanks, Elf!"

The *next* time, Elf had brought back *another* old toothpaste top. It made *another* good little dish. Twig had set it —just so!—beside the other two, on the table. Then she had said, "Thanks, Elf!"

Now she wondered what Elf was going to bring back *this* time. She was sitting in the doorway watching for him. She watched and watched.

And finally, after a long time, she heard him whistling his careless little tune, away off. As he came nearer, his little tune grew louder. And pretty soon Twig saw him. She saw that he was *not* bringing another old toothpaste top. She saw that he was bringing quite a big thing this time. He was carrying it in his arms. It was so big that Twig couldn't see the top part of Elf at all. She could just see something bright yellow, with Elf's legs walking—underneath.

As Elf came nearer, Twig saw that the bright yellow thing had two parts. Yes, it had! The two parts were moving up and down, up and down, slowly, as Elf walked. What in the world could *this* be? Twig jumped up and ran as fast as she could, to see.

"Why, Elf!" she said as soon as she was close to him. "Why, *Elf!*" she whispered, stopping still as a statue.

It was a pair of wings—a pair of wings as yellow as Twig's Papa's taxi! And between them was a long black thing shaped very much like Twig's Mama's best black pin, which she always wore on Sundays—only this had *six* little points, instead of one, to fasten the wings on with.

"Where did you ever find them?" whispered Twig.

"Out in the alley," said Elf.

Twig reached up and touched them, very, very gently. "Could I . . . could I . . . try them on?" she whispered.

"Sure!" said Elf. "Turn round!"

So Twig turned round, while Elf fastened the wings, by the six little points, to the back of her dress. Then she turned round again, for Elf to see.

"How do I look?" she asked.

"You look the same as you always looked—" said Elf. "No different—except you've got wings on!"

"Honestly, Elf!" said Twig. "Run and bring the mirror, will you, please?"

So Elf ran into the house and out again, dragging the piece of shiny paper behind him. He held it up, while Twig turned round and round and round before it.

Meantime the wings had been moving up and down faster, as if they wanted to fly. Twig could see them in the mirror, moving faster and faster, behind her shoulders. They moved so fast that they pulled Twig up onto her tiptoes, and up . . . up some more, until she wasn't touching the ground at all! She waved good-bye to herself, in the mirror.

" 'Bye, Elf!" she squeaked.

And the next minute she was doing a little loop-the-loop, away up in the air.

The *next* minute she was up as high as the Sparrows' nest. She could see Mrs. Sparrow sitting there on her eggs.

"Hello, Mrs. Sparrow!" squeaked Twig.

"Bless my feathers!" said Mrs. Sparrow. "Who's that?"

"It's me!" squeaked Twig.

Mrs. Sparrow could hardly believe it. She cocked her head—this way. Then she cocked her head—that way. After a while she cocked her head—this way again. "Well, I never in all my life!" she said at last. "Where did you get those wings, little missy?"

"Elf found them," explained Twig, "out in the alley."

"Well, I declare!" said Mrs. Sparrow. "What next?" Then she began to chuckle.

Twig waved good-bye, and down she flew—right down to the stream—and dipped the toes of her shoes in drainpipe water. Up she flew again. "Look, Elf!" she squeaked, touching her toes to a dandelion leaf. "Elf, *look!*" she squeaked, touching her toes to the edge of the roof.

Over the roof she flew, and back again. She flew around in a great big circle.

Oh, wasn't *this* lovely? Wasn't it lovely having *wings?*

63

She waved her arms, very, very gracefully as she flew. " 'Fairies all,' " she said, " 'come dance tonight—every elf . . . and . . . every sprite!' "

Then down she dropped and touched her toes to the ground. "Would *you* like to try the wings on now, Elf?" she asked.

Would he! Elf began to jump up and down, very much excited. He could hardly wait to help Twig unfasten the six little points from the back of her dress. He could hardly wait for her to fasten them to the back of his potato-skin jacket. He turned around, but he wiggled so that Twig let go of the wings. And—

Up they flew, all by themselves . . . up . . . up . . . up . . . higher than Mrs. Sparrow's nest! Then they turned and flew across the back yard so fast that Twig had time only to squeak, "Oh, Elf! They're *going!*"—before they were gone, over the fence and away.

Twig and Elf watched and watched, to see whether they would fly back again.

"Well—" said Elf, when it really began to look as if they never would.

"Well, what?" asked Twig.

"Well, *well!*" said Elf, slipping his hands into his potato-skin pockets. Then he began to whistle his careless little tune.

Twig laid her hand on Elf's shoulder and whispered something into his ear. It couldn't be heard, because of the loudness of the little tune. But this is what she whispered:

"Thanks, Elf!"

ELF THE GREAT

TWIG WAS GOING UP to Mrs. Sparrow's nest, to keep her company while she sat on her eggs. But Elf didn't care to go, this time. He said he'd rather stay home by himself.

"All right, little missy!" said Mrs. Sparrow. "Hop on!"

So Twig hopped on Mrs. Sparrow's back. "Elf," she said, "sweep the floor for me while I'm gone, will you, please?" Then she had to hold both her hands over her mouth for a minute, to keep from laughing. It was a joke, of course. She didn't really expect him to sweep the floor!

Mrs. Sparrow chuckled. " 'Bye, little fellow!" she said, spreading her wings. "Up we go!" she chirped.

And up they went.

" 'Bye, Elf!" called Twig on the way.

" 'Bye!" called Elf, standing near the dandelion, with his hands in his potato-skin pockets.

67

He watched until Twig and Mrs. Sparrow had lighted safely on the edge of the nest. Now! He was all by himself! He could do anything he wanted to! Quickly he took his hands from his pockets. He caught hold of the dandelion's stalk, and climbed up. The stalk bent over toward the roof of the little house. Elf jumped to the roof. He lay down on the roof, flat on his back, and stretched out his legs.

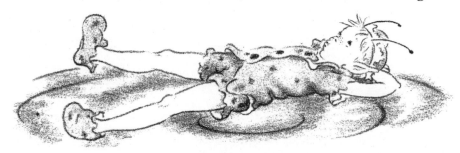

He looked up at the sky and whistled his careless little tune, twice over. Then he pulled himself to the edge of the roof and looked down. He was right above the doorway. He could see Mrs. Sparrow's feather standing in its place there. He remembered what Twig had said—about sweeping the floor. He whistled his careless little tune some more, looking down at the broom. At last he had an idea! The floor was going to be swept. But not by him. No, indeed! The floor was going to be swept by *magic!*

Elf rolled himself over, hung by his hands from the edge of the roof, and let himself down. He ran into the house and out again, with his book. He sat down, cross-legged, in the doorway, opened his book and turned to the back. He ran his finger quickly down. Then he turned to page one hundred. After a while he slapped the book shut. He stood up and folded his arms in front of him, grandly.

"Floor," he said, "sweep yourself!"

Nothing happened.

"I say—sweep yourself!"

Nothing happened.

"Sweep—I say!"

Still nothing happened.

"Floor," said Elf, "I'm about to give you one more chance! I'm about to say some very powerful words!" And he said them, "Floor, floor—sweep yourself! Thr-r-ree, four —this is Elf! Seven, eight—*Elf the Great!* Eleven, twelve— THE GREAT ELF!"

Bing-bing-bing!—out came the bottletop, on its edge. *Rumpety bump!*—out rolled the thimble. *Thump! Thump! Thump!*—out hopped the three toothpaste tops, one after another. *Swish!*—the mirror came flying out.

Elf the Great swung his arms forward and pointed all his fingers at the sparrow-feather broom. *Whee!* It was as if the little house had sucked the broom in through the door. *Wiggle-waggle!*—the broom began sweeping.

69

Poof! Out came a cloud of dust. *Poof!* Out came another. "*K-choo!*" sneezed Elf the Great.

Poof! Poof! Clouds of dust kept coming.

Swish-swoop! The mirror flew back and forth, around the house, around the dandelion, around the house, around the dandelion. *Swish-swoop!* It made a figure eight. *Thump! Thump! Thump!*—the three toothpaste tops went hopping all over the place. Around the dandelion rolled the bottle-top—*bing-bing-bing!*—on its edge. Around the house rolled the thimble—*bumpety-bump!*

Elf the Great ran to the dandelion and climbed its stalk again. Again he jumped to the roof.

He stood on the roof, waving his arms and squeaking, "Yippee! *Yippee!* YIPPEE!"

And, just at that moment, down flew Twig and Mrs. Sparrow, from the nest.

"Elf, for goodness sakes!" said Twig. "What's going on here?"

Elf the Great folded his arms in front of him, grandly, and stepped to the edge of the roof. "*K-choo!*" he sneezed.

Mrs. Sparrow began to chuckle. She just couldn't help it. She shook so with chuckling that Twig fell off her back.

Bing-bing-bing! came the bottletop. It bumped into Twig. "Ouch!" said Twig.

70

The thimble came rolling. One of the toothpaste tops came hopping. Twig tried to catch it, but—*thump!*—it hopped away. *Swish-swoop!*—the mirror came flying. Twig ducked her head. *Poof! Poof!* came the clouds of dust.

71

"Elf! Come down from there this minute, and—*k-choo!*—and—*k-choo!*—stop this!" called Twig.

Elf the Great let himself down from the roof. He stepped to the doorway, in the midst of the clouds of dust. "Floor," he said, "stop sweeping yourself!"

Nothing stopped.

"Stop—I say!" said Elf the Great.

Still nothing stopped. The broom kept right on going *wiggle-waggle* inside the house. The clouds of dust kept right on coming out. The thimble and the bottletop kept right on rolling, around and around. The toothpaste tops kept right on hopping up and down. The mirror kept right on flying back and forth. Mrs. Sparrow kept right on chuckling.

Suddenly Twig ran into the house and out again, with Mrs. Sparrow's feather. "Now, stop!" she said, standing it in its place by the door. "And *I* mean it!"

Bump! The thimble stopped rolling. The bottletop made a little circle and fell down flat. The toothpaste tops took three last little hops and were still. The mirror floated to the ground. The clouds of dust died slowly down.

"And *now,* Elf the Great," said Twig, with her hands on her hips, "you can just fix everything the way it was before!"

So, very, very meekly, Elf the Great did.

★

MRS. SPARROW'S CHILDREN

TWIG AND ELF WERE SITTING in the doorway, talking about Mrs. Sparrow and wondering how she was, when they heard a *whirr-r-r-r!*—and there she stood.

She looked very much worried. "Little fellow—little missy," she said, "how would you like to do something for me?"

"Oh, Mrs. Sparrow! We'd like to very much!" said Twig and Elf, both together, jumping up. "What is it?"

Mrs. Sparrow cocked her head—this way—while she thought what to say. Then she cocked her head—that way. After a while she cocked her head—this way again. "I don't like to mention my little troubles," she said at last, "but I might as well tell you—Sparrow's been gone ever since yesterday!"

73

"Ever since yesterday!" said Twig, and her mouth went wide open.

"Where in the world did he go?" asked Elf.

"I really don't know, little fellow," said Mrs. Sparrow, "and I wouldn't be so worried if it weren't for the children, but . . . well . . . I was just wondering, little fellow—little missy, if you'd mind sitting on the eggs while I go *once more* and try to find him."

"Oh! We wouldn't mind a bit, Mrs. Sparrow!" said Twig and Elf.

"Thanks, little missy—little fellow," said Mrs. Sparrow. "Hop right on, will you, please?"

So they hopped right on Mrs. Sparrow's back. And without so much as an "Up we go!"—up they went.

As soon as they lighted on the edge of the nest, Twig and Elf hopped right off Mrs. Sparrow's back and slid in. Then there was a *whirr-r-r-r!*—and away she flew. She seemed to be in quite a hurry.

"Which egg are *you* going to sit on?" asked Elf.

"This one!" said Twig, already on it.

So Elf sat down on another.

"Mrs. Sparrow said something about some children, didn't she?" said Elf after a while. "Whose children was she talking about?"

"*Her* children," said Twig.

"Her children?" asked Elf. "Where are *they?*"

"Inside the eggs," said Twig.

"What eggs?" asked Elf.

"*These* eggs," said Twig.

"Do you mean to say that Mrs. Sparrow's children are inside *these* eggs—*now?*" asked Elf, very much surprised.

"Of course!" said Twig. "That's why we're sitting on them. So they'll hatch!"

"Hatch?" said Elf. "What's that?"

Twig took a deep breath. Then she said, very slowly and patiently, "Honestly, Elf! Don't . . . you . . . know . . . anything . . . about . . . eggs? When the children are ready, they wiggle and wiggle and peck and peck and pretty soon—they come out, that's all."

Quickly Elf jumped up and looked back at the egg he had just been sitting on, as if he expected it to *explode.*

"Don't act so silly, Elf!" said Twig. "Hatching takes a long, long time. That's what Mrs. Sparrow told me. So sit down!"

Elf sat slowly down again, this time on another egg.

They sat and they sat and they sat.

"What are you thinking about?" asked Twig after a long, long time.

"Hm?" asked Elf.

"I say—what are you *thinking about?*"

"I'm thinking about magic," said Elf. "The way I used to, when I was sitting on the sack of potatoes, down in Old Shoemaker's cellar."

"What kind of magic did you used to think about?" asked Twig.

"Oh, no special kind," said Elf. "I just used to think what fun it would be if I could make all the potatoes jump out of the sack and go dancing around Old Shoemaker's cellar!"

"D-d-d-d-dancing around!" said Twig. Her egg had just begun to jiggle in a queer sort of way. "Who ever heard of p-p-p-p-potatoes d-d-d-d-dancing around?"

Elf's egg had begun to jiggle, too. "S-s-s-say!" he said. "M-m-m-m-my egg m-m-m-must b-b-b-be hatch-hatch-

hatching!" And the very next minute he fell off his egg, waving his arms and kicking his legs. "Help!" he squeaked.

"Help!" squeaked Twig, falling off *her* egg.

Then—

Crack! . . . Crack! . . . Crack! . . . Crack! went Mrs. Sparrow's four perfectly beautiful eggs. And—

One . . . two . . . three . . . four purplish heads came out, with purplish bulges at the sides of them and big bills which were yellow— Oh! They were as yellow as Twig's Papa's taxi. And—

One . . . two . . . three . . . four long scrawny necks came out. And—

One . . . two . . . three . . . four big purplish bodies came out, with little black pimples all over them and little skinny wings folded up at the sides.

Right away Mrs. Sparrow's children began to push and push and to crowd and crowd.

"Ouch!" squeaked Twig. "They're squashing me!"

"Me too!" squeaked a little voice from somewhere underneath.

Mrs. Sparrow's children kept pushing and pushing and crowding and crowding until they were all mixed up with one another. And Twig and Elf were all mixed up with them. It was as if somebody had taken a big spoon and stirred everything round and round and round in Mrs. Sparrow's nest.

After a good deal of pushing and crowding, Elf found himself at the side of the nest. He caught hold of the head of a big old safety pin and pulled himself up. Then he reached down and caught hold of Twig's arm and pulled her up, too.

"Whew!" said Elf, sitting on the edge of the nest, at last. "It's a wonder we're still alive!"

Twig looked down at Mrs. Sparrow's children, still pushing and pushing and crowding and crowding, down in the nest. "I don't think Mrs. Sparrow's children are very polite!" she said. "Do you?"

But Elf didn't have a chance to say what he thought, for just then Mrs. Sparrow's children stretched their four long scrawny necks and opened their four big yellow bills so wide that Twig and Elf could see all the way down their throats.

"*Squa-a-a-a-w-w-w-k!*" they yelled, in one loud voice, together.

"They're hungry!" said Twig. "*Now* what'll we do?"

Elf knew of only one thing to do. He stood up on the edge of the nest, put his hands to his mouth, and called as loud as he could, "*Mrs. Sparrow!*"

Twig stood up on the edge of the nest, too, and put *her* hands to *her* mouth and called as loud as *she* could, "*Mrs. Sparrow!*"

"*Squa-a-a-a-w-w-w-k! Squa-a-a-a-w-w-w-k!*" yelled Mrs. Sparrow's children.

"*Mrs. Sparrow!*" called Twig and Elf.

"*Squa-a-a-a-w-w-w-k! Squa-a-a-a-w-w-w-k!*"

"*Mrs. Sparrow!*"

"SQUA-A-A-W-W-W-K!"

"MRS. SPARROW! *Help!*"

It was quite a concert.

★

OLD BOY, THE ICE-WAGON HORSE

TWIG AND ELF WERE SITTING in the doorway, watching Mrs. Sparrow flying back and forth, back and forth, with crumbs and seeds and bugs and worms—for the children.

"Honestly!" said Twig. "The things those children eat!"

Mrs. Sparrow couldn't seem to find enough for them. She had to keep flying back and forth, back and forth, bringing things and going to look for more. And, all the while, her children kept up a continuous *Squa-a-a-w-w-w-k!* *Squa-a-a-w-w-w-k!* in the nest.

"Mrs. Sparrow looks tired," said Twig. "Doesn't she?"

No answer.

"I wish she'd found Sparrow," said Twig. "Don't you?"

No answer.

"Sparrow ought to be here to help her," said Twig. "Oughtn't he?"

No answer.

"Mrs. Sparrow hasn't got time to go looking for him any more now, has she?" said Twig.

No answer.

"Where in the world do you suppose Sparrow is?" said Twig.

No answer.

"Elf! For goodness sakes!" said Twig, poking him. "Why don't you say something? It's like talking to myself!"

"Hm?" asked Elf.

"Didn't you hear me talking?"

"No," said Elf.

"Why not?" asked Twig.

"I was having an idea," said Elf.

"An idea!" said Twig. "About what?"

"About *us* going to find Sparrow!" said Elf.

"Us!" said Twig. "How could we?"

Elf lifted his shoulders, several times. "I don't know!" he said. "That's as far as my idea got!"

Twig was quiet for a minute. Then she said, *"I know! We could ask Old Boy, the ice-wagon horse, to take us!"*

"Whew!" said Elf. "Old Boy, the ice-wagon horse!"

"That's what I said," said Twig. "What's the matter with Old Boy, the ice-wagon horse?"

"Well," said Elf, "he's—rather *big,* don't you think?"

"The bigger the better!" said Twig, jumping up. "Come on!"

So Elf jumped up, too. And they started off together, in the direction of the garbage can. They walked and they walked and they walked. And finally, after a long time, they got there. They waved to Old Girl, the cat, on top of the garbage can. Then they turned round the end of the fence into the alley.

And there, as still as a huge statue, stood Old Boy, the ice-wagon horse, sound asleep, as usual. Twig and Elf had to walk and walk to get to the front part of him. Then Twig stepped to his big front hoof and knocked on it.

"Old Boy!" she called.

Elf stepped to his other big front hoof and knocked on *it.* "Hoo hoo! Old Boy!" he called.

But Old Boy did not hear.

Twig and Elf *pounded* on both his big front hoofs. "Old Boy! Hoo hoo! Wake up!" they called.

But Old Boy neither heard nor felt them.

"Honestly!" said Twig, looking away up at Old Boy's big closed eye. "What'll we do?"

Elf looked up at Old Boy's other big closed eye. "If we could only get near to where his ears are!" said Elf.

84

"*I* know!" said Twig. "Let's climb his tail!"

"All right!" said Elf.

So they started off toward the other end of Old Boy. They walked and they walked and they walked. And finally they got to the place where Old Boy's long, long tail hung almost all the way down to the ground.

First Elf took hold and began to climb, hand over hand, up Old Boy's tail. Then Twig took hold and began to climb, hand over hand, up after him.

They climbed and they climbed.

"Come on!" said Elf when they got to the top.

So they walked along on Old Boy's broad back, jumping over the places where the harness was; running up and down the little hills where Old Boy's bones grew, underneath. Then they went wading through the hair of Old Boy's mane, all the way up his neck.

85

"Whew! Here we are at last!" said Elf, stepping around in front of Old Boy's big soft ear.

Twig stepped around in front of Old Boy's other big soft ear. "All right!" she said. "Call!"

So they both called, as loud as they could, *"Old Bo-o-oy!"* —right into his ears.

PPPPPPPPPPPPPPPP! sneezed Old Boy, all of a sudden. It shook so that Twig and Elf would surely have fallen off had they not had hold of Old Boy's big soft ears.

"Hello, Old Boy!" called Twig. It was like talking into a big telephone. *"Mrs. Sparrow's got four children!"*

"Mrs. Sparrow's very tired!" called Elf. *"She needs Sparrow to help her!"*

"We've got to find Sparrow!" called Twig. *"Will you take us, Old Boy?"*

All of a sudden Old Boy sneezed again—*PPPPPPPP PPPPPPPP!* And this time it shook so that Twig and Elf fell forward, each into one of Old Boy's big soft ears.

Twig turned around in her ear, and sat up. "Elf!" she squeaked. "We're going!"

And, sure enough, they were. They could hear the huge ice wagon rumbling along behind.

Elf turned around in *his* ear, and stretched out his legs. "Say! Mine's comfortable!" he called. "How's yours?"

"Mine's fine!" called Twig. "It's like riding in a rocking chair. Isn't it?"

"Hmmmmmmmmm?" asked Elf, yawning.

"I say—it's like—oh-ho-ho-hmmm!" yawned Twig. "Oh-ho-ho-hmmmm!" she yawned again. Then she leaned forward and looked over at Elf. "Elf!" she called. "Are you *asleep?*"

Elf didn't answer. His head was bobbing up and down. And his eyes were tight shut.

"Oh-ho-ho-ho-hmmmm!" yawned Twig, leaning back again. "Oh-ho-ho-ho-hmmmmmm!" she kept yawning. She just couldn't help it. Then she curled up her legs. "Oh-ho-ho-ho-hmmmmm!" she yawned once more. And the next minute *she* was asleep.

Old Boy was asleep, too. He had worked all his life, poor Old Boy. He was very tired. He slept while he was standing up or while he was walking along. Also he was very dusty. That made him sneeze.

PPPPPPPPPPPPPPPP! he sneezed.

And it shook so that they all woke up. But as soon as they woke up, they all went to sleep again.

Old Boy's sleepiness surely was catching!

SPARROW

MRS. SPARROW'S CHILDREN were asleep, too. They had had enough to eat, for a while!

Mrs. Sparrow was sitting on the edge of the nest, resting herself and looking up into the sky. She looked and looked. And pretty soon she saw a little speck, away off, over the city.

Mrs. Sparrow sat watching the little speck. She cocked her head—this way—watching it. Then she cocked her head —that way—watching it. After a while she cocked her head —this way again—watching the little speck. And pretty soon the little speck began to grow bigger. It kept growing bigger and bigger until it didn't look like a little speck at all, any more. It looked quite like a bird. Then it kept looking more and more like a bird, until Mrs. Sparrow could see that it *was* a bird. And after a while she saw that the bird was Sparrow, coming home!

"Well, it's about time!" said Mrs. Sparrow to herself. Then she said, "Why, bless my feathers! Who's that on his back?"

Sitting very gracefully on Sparrow's back was a little lady in a long pink dress. As Sparrow came nearer, Mrs. Sparrow could see that the little lady had bright yellow hair. As Sparrow came still nearer, Mrs. Sparrow could see that the little lady had wings. And around her neck she had a smart little fluffy brown fur. And on top of her head she had something round and shiny like a crown.

"Quite a beauty!" said Mrs. Sparrow to herself. "Quite a beauty! I wonder where he picked *her* up!"

Down from the sky swooped Sparrow, with the little lady's long pink dress trailing out behind him. "CHUP CHUP CHUP!" he shrieked, in his loud voice, as he sailed over the fence. "CHUP CHUP CHUP!" he shrieked, tipping his wings and gliding around in a big half-circle. "CHUP CHUP CHUP!" he shrieked, skimming along the ground and making his landing—right before the doorway of Twig's little house. Then he shouted, "WELL! THIS IS IT!"

Mrs. Sparrow saw the little lady clasp her hands and look around, very much delighted. "How lovely!" she heard her say. Then Mrs. Sparrow saw the little lady step gracefully from Sparrow's back and walk over toward the dandelion, swinging a little green bag which hung over her arm.

"I wonder who she is!" said Mrs. Sparrow to herself. "I think I'll just drop down and see!"

So down she dropped, and landed right between Sparrow and the little lady.

"HELLO THERE, SWEETIE PIE!" shouted Sparrow, so loud that the little lady had to put her hands up to her ears.

"Sweetie Pie indeed!" said Mrs. Sparrow. "Where have you been?"

"WHERE'VE I BEEN? CHUP CHUP CHUP!" shrieked Sparrow. "JUST TAKE A LOOK AT THE LITTLE LADY HERE, AND I'LL GIVE YOU THREE GUESSES WHERE I'VE BEEN!"

Mrs. Sparrow looked at the little lady. The little lady looked at Mrs. Sparrow. Her eyes were bright blue. "How do you do?" she said, smiling very sweetly.

"How-do, ma'am!" said Mrs. Sparrow.

"CHUP CHUP CHUP!" shrieked Sparrow. "NOW GUESS WHO THE LITTLE LADY IS!"

"That's easy," said Mrs. Sparrow, cocking her head. "She's a fairy."

"YOU'RE GETTING WARM," shouted Sparrow. "GUESS AGAIN! WHAT'S HER NAME?"

"How should I know?" said Mrs. Sparrow. "I never saw her before!"

"WELL, TAKE A GOOD LOOK NOW," shouted Sparrow. "THIS LITTLE LADY IS THE FAIRY QUEEN!"

The Fairy Queen!

Mrs. Sparrow had to spread her wings for a minute to keep from falling right over. Her bill went open and shut, open and shut, several times. Then she said, "Why, *ma'am!*" and made a little curtsy as best she could. "Well, I declare!" she said. "How did *Sparrow* ever—"

"Sparrow flew all the way to Fairyland," explained the Queen, "to find a fairy for Twig."

Out puffed the feathers on Sparrow's chest—and he began to strut proudly up and down, shrieking, "CHUP CHUP CHUP! NO ONE BUT THE QUEEN! NO ONE BUT THE FAIRY QUEEN WAS GOOD ENOUGH FOR TWIGGIE! CHUP CHUP CHUP! NO ONE BUT THE QUEEN!... BY THE WAY," he shouted, "WHERE IS TWIGGIE?"

"Why, I don't know!" said Mrs. Sparrow, very much surprised, looking all around. "She was here a while ago."

And just at that moment there was a loud *Squa-a-a-w-w-w-w-k!* from the nest.

"WHAT IN THE NAME OF COMMON SENSE IS THAT?" shouted Sparrow.

"That? Oh—that's the children," explained Mrs. Sparrow.

"CHILDREN?" shouted Sparrow, very much surprised. "WHOSE CHILDREN?"

"Our children," explained Mrs. Sparrow.

"OUR CHILDREN!" shouted Sparrow, so loud that the Queen had to put her hands up to her ears again. "WHY DIDN'T YOU TELL ME THIS BEFORE, SWEETIE PIE? CHUP CHUP CHUP CHUP CHUP CHUP CHUP! HOW MANY CHILDREN HAVE WE?"

"Four," said Mrs Sparrow, rather proudly. "All boys."

"FOUR LITTLE SPORTS!" shrieked Sparrow. "CHUP CHUP! LET'S HAVE A LOOK!'" He spread his wings. There was a WHIRR-R-R-R! And up to the nest he flew.

Mrs. Sparrow turned to the Queen. "Won't you have a seat, ma'am?" she asked politely.

"Thank you!" said the Queen, smiling and sitting down on one of the long green dandelion leaves.

"Won't you take off your fur, ma'am?" asked Mrs. Sparrow politely. "It's a hot day! Hotter than yesterday even!"

"Thank you!" said the Queen, smiling and taking off her smart little fluffy brown fur and laying it—just so!—on the leaf beside her.

"And now, if you'll pardon me, ma'am," said Mrs. Sparrow politely, "I think I'll fly up and see if the children are all right. Just make yourself at home, ma'am! The little missy won't be gone long, I'm sure!"

"Thank you!" said the Queen, smiling again.

Mrs. Sparrow spread her wings. And up she flew. "Well, I never in all my life!" she said to herself on the way. "What *next?*"

★

THE FAIRY QUEEN

P*PPPPPPPPPPPPPPPPP!* sneezed Old Boy, the ice-wagon horse.

And Twig opened her eyes. She peeked around the side of Old Boy's big soft ear. "Elf!" she squeaked. "We're not going any more!"

"Hm?" said Elf, sitting up in Old Boy's other big soft ear.

"Well, for goodness sakes!" said Twig, climbing out onto Old Boy's forehead. "Look where we are!"

Elf crawled out onto Old Boy's forehead, too. "Say!" he said. "What's the idea? We're right where we were before!"

And, sure enough, Old Boy was standing out in the alley, beside the fence, just as if he had never moved!

Elf scratched his head and looked all around. "What about Sparrow?" he said.

"What about him!" said Twig. "There he is!"

"Where?" asked Elf.

"Right over there!" said Twig, pointing.

And, sure enough, there he was, hopping about in the back yard, looking for things for the children to eat.

"I wonder when *he* got home!" said Twig. And then she said, "See? Old Boy's pretty smart, isn't he? We told him to take us to find Sparrow—didn't we?" She stepped to Old Boy's big soft ear and called, *"Thanks, Old Bo-o-oy!"* as loud as she could. Then she pulled herself up over Old Boy's forehead. "Come on, Elf!" she said. "Let's go home!"

So Elf pulled *him*self up over Old Boy's forehead, too. And together they went wading through the hair of Old Boy's mane, all the way down his neck. They went walking along on Old Boy's broad back, jumping over the places where the harness was; running up and down the little hills where Old Boy's bones grew, underneath. Then they went sliding down Old Boy's long, long tail to the ground.

"Come on, Elf!" said Twig, turning round the end of the fence into the back yard.

So Elf followed, whistling his careless little tune.

"Oh—doesn't Old Girl look *beautiful* up there?" said Twig, pointing to the top of the garbage can.

"She doesn't look any more beautiful than she ever looked," said Elf.

"Well, maybe it's just that I'm so glad to see her," said Twig.

And on they walked. They walked and they walked. And finally, after a long time, they got to the place where Sparrow was hopping about on the ground.

"Hello, Sparrow!" said Twig.

Sparrow looked up. "WHO IN THE NAME OF COMMON SENSE ARE YOU?" he shouted. And then he shrieked, "WELL, IF IT ISN'T TWIGGIE! CHUP CHUP CHUP! TWIGGIE! POOR LITTLE TWIGGIE! WHAT'S HAPPENED TO YOU?"

"Nothing," said Twig, looking down at herself . "Why?"

"WHY!" shouted Sparrow. "YOU'RE NOT QUITE AS BIG AS YOU USED TO BE!"

"Oh," said Twig. "That's just—magic. Elf did it! *This* is Elf!" she said, pointing to him.

"HELLO THERE, LITTLE SPORT!" shouted Sparrow. "PLEASED TO MEET YOU! . . . SAY, TWIGGIE! BY THE WAY —THERE'S A LITTLE LADY HERE TO SEE YOU!"

"A little lady? To see *me?*" said Twig. "Who is she?"

"WHO IS SHE? CHUP CHUP CHUP CHUP CHUP!" shrieked Sparrow.

Out puffed the feathers on his chest. "JUST FOLLOW ME!" he shouted. And away he hopped, in the direction of the little house.

So Twig and Elf went walking along in that direction, too.

"Oh—doesn't our house look *beautiful,* over there?" said Twig, pointing to it.

"It doesn't look any more beautiful than it ever looked," said Elf.

"Well, maybe it's just that I'm so glad to be home," said Twig.

And on they walked.

"HERE SHE COMES! HERE SHE COMES!" shouted Sparrow, hopping on ahead.

And *then* . . .

Out from behind the dandelion stepped a beautiful little lady, with a long pink dress on, and hair that was as yellow as Twig's Papa's taxi, and wings you could see right through —like cellophane.

Out she stepped, with a little green bag hung over her arm and a shiny crown that looked just like Twig's Mama's wedding ring, on the top of her head. My, but she was beautiful! She was as beautiful as a flower! She smiled, and came hurrying to meet them.

"TWIGGIE!" shouted Sparrow as soon as the little lady came close. *Away out* puffed the feathers on his chest. "TWIGGIE," he shouted, "THIS LITTLE LADY IS—"

The little lady smiled very sweetly.

Twig smiled very sweetly, too.

"THE . . . FAIRY . . . QUEEN!" shouted Sparrow, so loud that his words kept coming back and coming back from all over.

The . . . Fairy . . . Queen!

The . . . Fairy . . . Queen!

Twig's mouth went wide open and stayed that way for quite a while. So, for quite a while, she couldn't say anything. She looked over at Elf. Elf's eyes were as big as toothpaste tops! She looked back at the Queen. The Queen was smiling at them both, very sweetly.

"O-o-o-o-oh, no!" said Twig, at last, shaking her head.

"I know what this is! This is a dream! *I* know why every-thing looks so beautiful! Everything always looks beautiful —in dreams. O-o-oh, no!" she said, shaking her head again. "I'm asleep! I'm not here! I'm still asleep in Old Boy's ear, and this is just a dream!"

"CHUP CHUP CHUP CHUP CHUP CHUP CHUP!" shriek-ed Sparrow. "PINCH HER, LITTLE SPORT! PINCH HER!"

"No!" squeaked Twig, running round the dandelion with Elf after her. "No! I don't *want* to wake up! Elf! Stop! Oh, Elf . . . *ouch!*"

Twig stopped still as a statue. She turned her head to look. Why! She wasn't in Old Boy's ear at all! . . . There stood Sparrow! . . . There stood Elf! . . . Slowly, slowly, Twig turned her head to see if the Fairy Queen was standing there, too. . . . She was!

And just at that moment there was a loud *Squa-a-a-w-w-w-k!* from the nest.

"HEAR THAT, TWIGGIE?" shouted Sparrow. "THAT'S NO DREAM, I CAN TELL YOU!"

And Sparrow began hopping about on the ground once more, looking for things for the children to eat.

★

IN HONOR OF THE QUEEN

"ELF!" WHISPERED TWIG. "Run to the garbage can and ask Old Girl, the cat, to give a concert, right away—will you, please?"

"A concert!" said Elf. "Why?"

"Don't you know who's visiting us?" whispered Twig.

"Sure!" said Elf.

"Well?" whispered Twig.

"Well, what?" asked Elf.

"Well, for goodness sakes!" whispered Twig. "It isn't *every* day we have a Queen here! We've got to give something in her honor!"

"Why?" asked Elf.

"Because . . . that's . . . what's . . . usually . . . done!" whispered Twig, very slowly and patiently. Then she whispered, "Go on, Elf! I'd go with you, only I have to stay here to keep Her Majesty company!"

"What'll I say?" asked Elf.

"Just ask Old Girl to give a concert!" whispered Twig.

"Will Old Girl know what I mean?" asked Elf.

"Of course! She often gives concerts! Just ask her to give one now, that's all. Just tell her that the Fairy Queen happens to be in this back yard!" whispered Twig grandly. "Go on, Elf! Will you, please?"

"All right!" said Elf. And away he ran, in the direction of the garbage can.

Twig skipped into the house. The Queen was standing before the mirror, fixing her crown.

"Your Majesty," said Twig, "there's going to be a concert! Would you like to come outside, to listen?"

"A concert! How lovely!" said the Queen.

Twig took the Queen's arm and they walked slowly out to the dandelion.

"Shall we sit here, Your Majesty?" said Twig, crawling underneath.

Very, very gracefully, the Queen crawled underneath, too.

"How lovely," she said, "being able to listen to a concert right in your own back yard! Do you often have concerts?"

"Yes, quite often, Your Majesty," said Twig. "In the middle of the night, mostly. But this one is a special concert!"

"When is this one going to begin?" asked the Queen.

"Oh—pretty soon," said Twig.

And, sure enough, pretty soon it did.

> Meeow!
> Meeooow!
> *Mee-e-o-o-o-w!*

The Queen looked all around. "How lovely!" she whispered. "Where is it coming from?"

"From the garbage can, Your Majesty!" whispered Twig.

"Who is singing?" whispered the Queen.

"Old Girl, the cat, Your Majesty!" whispered Twig.

And the concert went on.

> *Meeooow!*
> *Mee-o-o-o-o-w!*
> MEEE-O-O-O-W!
> MEEE-O-O-O-W!

After a while Elf came running back from the garbage can. He came sliding underneath the dandelion. "Whew!"

he said, rather out of breath, sitting down on the other side of the Queen. "Am I—late?"

"*Sh!*" whispered Twig, leaning forward and shaking her head at Elf. "Keep quiet!" she whispered. Then she leaned back again.

And the concert went on.

Mee-o-o-o-w-w-w!

Meee-o-ooo-o-o-w-w-w!

Mee-o-o-ow!

MEEE-E-E-E-O-O-O-W-W-W!

"Old Girl can surely sing, can't she, Your Majesty?" asked Elf.

"*Sh!*" whispered Twig, leaning forward again and shaking her head. "Keep quiet!"

And the concert went on.

Mee-o-o-o-w-w-w-w!

Meeee-o-ooo-o-o-oo-w-w!

Meeeee-o-o-oo-w-w-w-w!

MEEE-E-E-E-O-O-W!

The Queen leaned her head back against the dandelion's stalk and closed her eyes.

Twig smiled, proudly, to herself. Old Girl had never sung like *this* before!

"This concert is being given in *your honor,* Your Majesty!" said Elf, giving the Queen's dress a little tug.

"Is it—really?" asked the Queen, opening her eyes and looking from Twig to Elf and back again. *"Really?"*

Twig nodded her head, smiling very proudly. Yes, it really was!

"How lovely!" whispered the Queen.

And the concert went on.

Mee-ee-ee-e-e-e-o-o-o-w!

Meee-o-o-o-o-eee-e-o-o-w!

Meeee-e-e-e-e-o-o-o-ow!

MEEOW!

The dandelion leaves quivered, the stick-of-gum bridge jiggled, the little house and everything in it rattled, as Old Girl, the cat, filled the whole back yard with music.

Mee-e-o-o-o-ow!

Mee-o-e-o-o-o-ow!

Mee-e-o-o-o-o-ow!

Meee-o-o-ooo-oow!

MEEEE-E-E-EEE-OO-O-OW!

MEEEEEEE-EEE-O-O-O-OW!

"How lovely!" whispered the Queen once more, leaning her head back against the dandelion's stalk and closing her eyes.

She was very, *very* polite!

★

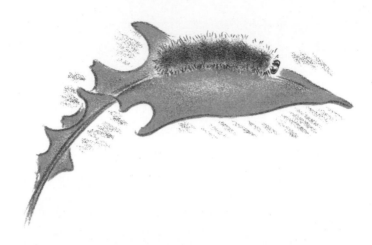

THE QUEEN'S FUR

TWIG AND THE QUEEN had gone to the garbage can to thank Old Girl, the cat, for giving such a lovely concert. Elf was home, by himself.

He was sitting in the doorway with his little red book open on his lap. But he wasn't looking at his book. He was looking at the Queen's smart little fluffy brown fur, which lay on the leaf—where the Queen had put it. Twig had told Elf NOT to touch it!

Suddenly Elf slapped his book shut. He jumped up and ran to the dandelion to look at the fur more closely. He looked and looked. But he didn't touch it.

"Here, kitty-kitty-kitty!" called Elf. Surely there was no harm in talking to it!

"Kitty-kitty-kitty!" called Elf softly. And—

The Queen's smart little fluffy brown fur began to come to him, along the leaf.

"Whew!" said Elf to himself. He hadn't exactly expected it to do that!

Along the leaf and along the leaf it kept coming. It came all the way along the leaf, down to the ground.

Now what would it do? Would it come along the ground?

"Kitty-kitty-kitty!" called Elf.

And, sure enough, along the ground it came!

"Here, kitty-kitty-kitty!" called Elf, leading the way to the stick-of-gum bridge.

And the Queen's smart little fluffy brown fur followed him.

Now what would it do? Would it go across the bridge?

No, it wouldn't. It curled itself up into a fluffy brown ball.

"Kitty-kitty-kitty!" called Elf. "Come on!" And he walked across the bridge.

Pretty soon the fur uncurled itself and walked across, too. *Now* what would it do?

"Kitty-kitty-kitty!" called Elf, leading the way in a straight line.

And the fur followed in a straight line. Would it follow in a zigzag?

"Kitty-kitty-kitty!" called Elf, leading the way in a zigzag.

And the fur followed.

Would it follow in a circle?

"Kitty-kitty-kitty!" called Elf, leading the way in a big round circle.

And—the fur followed.

Would it follow in a figure eight?

"Kitty-kitty-kitty!" called Elf, leading the way in a big figure eight.

But just then the fur started to lead the way itself, in a straight line, slowly but surely, toward the drainpipe.

"Here, kitty-kitty-kitty!" called Elf. "Don't go there!"

But the Queen's smart little fluffy brown fur paid no attention. It kept right on leading the way, in a straight line, slowly but surely, toward the drainpipe.

So Elf followed.

And finally, after a long time, the Queen's fur got to the drainpipe.

Now what would it do?

It began to go up the drainpipe.

"Oh, kitty!" called Elf. "I don't think you should go up there!"

But the Queen's smart little fluffy brown fur paid no attention. On up the drainpipe it went.

Elf really thought he ought to take it down. But he couldn't touch it, because Twig had told him NOT to.

Up...up the drainpipe it went, until it was up higher than Elf's head.

"Kitty-kitty-kitty!" Elf kept calling "Kitty-kitty! *Please* come down!"

But it would not come down.

Up...up...up the drainpipe it went. Now it was higher than Elf could reach.... Now it was higher than Elf could jump....Now it was so high that Elf could hardly see it.... Now it was gone.

Oh! Oh!

Would it ever come down?

Elf waited . . . and waited . . . and waited. But it did not come down.

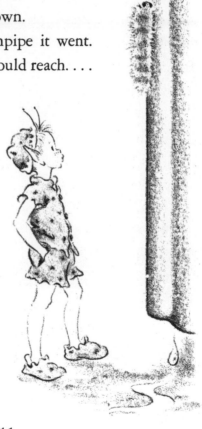

Then Elf turned around and began to walk slowly home.

What would Twig say?

What would *the Queen* say?

Elf walked as slowly as he could. He walked in zigzags and circles and figure eights and squares and triangles and potato shapes—oh! he walked in all sorts of shapes, for he didn't exactly want to get home right away.

He was walking, very slowly, in a big wiggly potato shape, when he happened to look up. And there he saw Twig, standing on the other side of the stream with her hands on her hips.

Very slowly Elf finished his big wiggly potato shape. He slipped his hands into his potato-skin pockets and began to whistle his careless little tune. He walked to the stream and jumped across it.

"Well?" asked Twig, with her hands on her hips.

"Well what?" asked Elf. "When did *you* get home?"

"Quite a while ago," said Twig. "Where is it?"

"Where is what?" asked Elf.

"You know what!" said Twig.

"You mean—the Queen's fur?" asked Elf.

"That's just what I mean," said Twig.

Elf lifted his shoulders several times. "I don't know!" he said.

"I thought I told you NOT to touch it!" said Twig.

"I didn't touch it!" said Elf.

"You did!" said Twig. "It couldn't have gone away by itself, could it?"

"Yes, it could!" said Elf.

"Honestly, Elf!" said Twig. "That's not funny!"

"Really it did!" said Elf.

"It did not!" said Twig.

"It *did!*"

"It did not!"

And just at that moment the Queen came out of the house. "Twig! Elf!" she said. "Please don't talk to each other like that!"

"Elf took your fur, Your Majesty!" said Twig.

"I did not!" said Elf. "I tell you it went away by itself!"

"That's perfectly all right, Elf," said the Queen, smiling and patting him on the shoulder. "I expected it to."

"You *expected* it to!" said Twig, very much surprised. "Well, for goodness sakes, Your Majesty! What kind of a fur was it?"

"Caterpillar," said the Queen.

★

THE ROYAL MAGICAL COBB-WEBB KERCHIEF

INSIDE THE HOUSE, Twig was showing her three tooth-paste tops to the Queen. "And the *next* time, Elf brought me *this* one!" she was saying, proudly, when she heard Elf calling, from outside. She ran to the doorway.

"What is it?" she asked.

"A cloud!" said Elf, standing with his hands in his potato-skin pockets and his head tipped back.

Twig stepped outside and tipped her head back too. "That's no cloud!" she said. "Who ever heard of a square cloud?"

And just then the Queen stepped outside.

"Your Majesty," said Twig, "what in the world do you suppose *that* is?"

The Queen held on to her crown, to keep it from falling off, while she tipped *her* head back *too*. "Why!" she said. "That's the Royal Magical Cobb-Webb Kerchief! Lord Buzzle Cobb-Webb must be coming after me. He always comes after me," she explained.

"How does he know you're here?" asked Twig.

114

"He knows—by magic," explained the Queen.

"Magic!" squeaked Elf, very much interested. *"Who* did you say was coming?"

"Lord Buzzle Cobb-Webb," said the Queen. "He's a great magician."

"A great magician! Coming *here!"* queaked Elf. "Yippee!"

"I can't see him!" said Twig.

The Queen held on to her crown, to keep it from falling off, while she tipped her head back again. "He's sitting on top of the Kerchief," she explained. "We'll see him after a while."

Down . . . down . . . down floated the Royal Magical Cobb-Webb Kerchief. And, sure enough, after a while they

saw a high hat with little dents in it, all over, like the dents all over the garbage can. The hat looked as though there had been a good many things put into it and taken out of it in its day. Then, after another while, they saw two arms waving in the air. And, after *another* while, they saw that the high hat and the two arms belonged to a little old gentleman with fluffy white hair and a pair of gold-rimmed spectacles.

Down . . . down . . . down floated the Kerchief, with the little old gentleman sitting on it waving his arms. Down . . . down . . . down . . . all the way down it floated until, at last, it came to rest, very, very gently, on the ground.

"Yippee!" squeaked Elf, jumping over the stream. "Yippee!" he squeaked, running to meet the little old gentleman. "Whew!" he said, with his breath going in and out, in and out. "Are you—*really*—a great magician, sir?"

A piece of the little old gentleman's fluffy white hair came loose from his head and went floating away. He watched it go, through his gold-rimmed spectacles.

"*Sodosodasarsaparilla!*" he whispered.

"Hm?" asked Elf.

"Elf!" called the Queen. "You mustn't blow at Lord Buzzle! It makes him very cross to see his hair floating away! Now, help him up, Elf—will you, please?"

So Elf helped him up.

"Well well well well well well well!" said the little old gentleman hurrying forward, for now, through his gold-rimmed spectacles, he saw the Queen. But just as he came to the stick-of-gum bridge, he stubbed the toe of one of his long pointed shoes. "*Sodasodasarsaparilla!*" he whispered, again.

"Hm?" asked Elf.

"Elf!" called the Queen. "Take Lord Buzzle's arm and help him across the bridge—will you, please?"

So Elf took the little old gentleman's arm and helped him.

"There!" said the Queen, smiling very sweetly, when the little old gentleman was beside her, at last. "Now, Lord Buzzle, may I introduce Twig—"

The little old gentleman took off his high hat and made a low bow. "How do you do, young lady!" he said.

"How-do, Mr. Buzzle, sir!" said Twig, as politely as she could, because he was a great magician.

"—and Elf—" said the Queen.

The little old gentleman made another low bow. "How do you do, young whipper-snapper!" he said.

But all Elf could say was "Whew! . . . A great magician! . . . *Whew!*"

And *two* little pieces of Lord Buzzle's fluffy white hair came loose from his head and went floating away.

Oh-oh!

"Lord Buzzle!" said the Queen, quickly. "Where have you been?"

"At the Public Library," said Lord Buzzle. "Why?"

"Look at your elbow!" said the Queen.

So Lord Buzzle looked at his elbow, through his gold-rimmed spectacles.

"No, your other elbow!" said the Queen.

So Lord Buzzle looked at his other elbow, through his gold-rimmed spectacles. And there, sure enough, *was* his other elbow, sticking out through quite a big hole.

"I'll have to darn that hole, before it gets any bigger," said the Queen. "What were you *doing* at the Public Library?"

"Magic," said Lord Buzzle.

"Magic!" squeaked Elf. "What kind of magic?"

"Just plain, ordinary magic, young whipper-snapper," said Lord Buzzle. "On some plain, ordinary potatoes."

"Potatoes!" said the Queen, very much surprised. "What were potatoes doing at the Public Library?"

"They were—dancing," said Lord Buzzle.

"Dancing!" said the Queen. "I've never heard of such a thing! How did they happen to be doing that?"

"Oh—some young whipper-snapper started them," said Lord Buzzle, "and then—ran away."

Twig looked at Elf. His face was slowly changing from pink to pale red, from pale red to bright red, and his knees were going wobble-wobble. "Elf!" she whispered. "Are you—feeling all right?"

"Sure!" said Elf, with his face as red as the tomatoes in the pictures all round the little house, and his knees going wobble-wobble. "Why?"

"I just wondered," said Twig.

★

TWO VERY IMPORTANT CONVERSATIONS

THE QUEEN WAS SITTING on a leaf on one side of the dandelion, darning the hole in the elbow of Lord Buzzle Cobb-Webb's coat. Lord Buzzle Cobb-Webb was sitting on a leaf on the other side, in his shirt sleeves, waiting for the hole in the elbow of his coat to be darned.

At exactly the same moment, Twig came out from inside the house, with Mrs. Sparrow's feather, and Elf came out from behind the house, with his little red book. At exactly the same moment, Twig stood Mrs. Sparrow's feather in its place, by the door, and Elf began to walk, very slowly, in a big wiggly potato shape, around the dandelion to the other side. At exactly the same moment, Twig skipped to the leaf where the Queen was sitting and Elf came to the end of his big wiggly potato shape and stood before Lord Buzzle Cobb-Webb. Then two very important conversations took place, on each side of the dandelion, both at the same time. But they couldn't be written down on paper, both at the same time. The only way they could be written down on paper, was: first, one side—and then, the other.

"Hello, Your Majesty!" said Twig, climbing up beside the Queen.

"Hello, Twig!" said the Queen, taking a little stitch across the hole in the elbow of Lord Buzzle's coat.

Twig leaned away down close to look at the Queen's thread. She had never seen such a fine kind of thread. "What kind of thread is that, Your Majesty?" she asked.

"It's called Cobb-Webb thread, after Lord Buzzle," explained the Queen, taking a little stitch. "A good many things in Fairyland are called after him."

"Is that so?" said Twig, sitting up straight and folding her hands in her lap. "How long does it take to get to Fairyland, Your Majesty?"

"That depends on the way you go," said the Queen. "If you go the way Sparrow went, it takes a whole day to get there. If you go on the Royal Magical Cobb-Webb Kerchief, it takes only a few minutes."

"It must be beautiful in Fairyland!" said Twig.

"It is," said the Queen, taking another little stitch.

"Are there—trees?" asked Twig.

"Yes," said the Queen.

"And—flowers?" asked Twig.

"Yes," said the Queen.

"And—grass?" asked Twig.

"Yes," said the Queen.

"And—streams?" asked Twig.

"Yes," said the Queen, "streams and lakes and round blue ponds."

"Will you—will you—will you and Lord Buzzle have to be going back to Fairyland soon?" asked Twig.

"As soon as this hole is darned," said the Queen.

"Oh," said Twig, sadly.

But the Queen only smiled and took another little stitch. "How would you like to go with us?" she asked.

"Go—*with you! . . .* To—*Fairyland! . . .* How would I—*like to! . . .* Oh! *Your Majesty!*" squeaked Twig. "Do you *really mean it?*"

The Queen smiled again. Of course she really meant it.

"I'd like to very much!" said Twig, making the leaf move up and down, up and down, by giving little pushes against the ground, first with one foot and then with the other. Then, suddenly, she sat still as a statue. She looked down into her lap and her face turned quite pink, the way it did once when she was in a play, and her Mama and her Papa and a good many other mamas and papas were there. "I wish I didn't have this old dress on," she said.

"Why do you wish that?" asked the Queen.

"Well, who ever heard of going to Fairyland with a plain ordinary old dress on? Just look at it, Your Majesty!" said Twig. "And just look at these old shoes!"

The Queen looked at them and smiled. "They're only on the outside of you, Twig," she said. "It doesn't matter how plain or how ordinary or how old the things on the outside are, you know. It's what is inside that matters."

"Inside!" said Twig, very much surprised.

The Queen looked up at the little round bud at the top of the dandelion's stalk. "Do you know what is inside of that plain ordinary little round bud?" she asked.

"Yes, Your Majesty," answered Twig. "A beautiful flower."

"There's something just as beautiful inside of you," said the Queen.

"Something—*beautiful!* Inside of—*me!*" said Twig. "Honestly, Your Majesty! How *could* there be?"

"How could there be a beautiful flower inside of the little round bud?" asked the Queen.

Twig lifted her shoulders several times. "I don't know!" she said. "There just *is,* that's all."

"And there 'just *is*' something beautiful inside of you," said the Queen. "It's called imagination."

"Is that so?" said Twig. "What can it do?"

"It can do magic," said the Queen.

"Magic!" squeaked Twig. "What kind of magic?"

"Any kind of magic you wish," said the Queen.

"Well, for goodness sakes!" said Twig. She looked toward the other side of the dandelion where Elf and Lord Buzzle were sitting. She held both her hands over her mouth

for a minute, to keep from laughing. Then she leaned close to the Queen. "I don't think we'd better tell Elf—" she whispered, "about my—my—"

"I-ma-gi-na-tion?" said the Queen, very slowly and patiently. "Why not?"

"Oh," said Twig, sitting up straight again. "Just . . . because!" She folded her hands in her lap. Then she said, "Your Majesty, could Elf—could Elf—could Elf go to Fairyland, too?"

"Why, yes!" said the Queen, smiling very sweetly, "if

he'd like to. I think that would be a perfectly lovely end, don't you?"

"A perfectly lovely end—to what?" asked Twig.

"To the story," said the Queen, taking a little stitch.

"What story?" asked Twig.

"*This* story," said the Queen.

"Your Majesty!" said Twig, with her eyes nearly popping out of her head. "Do you mean to say that *we're* in a—*story?*"

"Why, yes," said the Queen. "Didn't you know we were?"

"Right now?" asked Twig. "Right this very minute?"

"Right this very minute," said the Queen.

"Is everything we say in it?" asked Twig. "Everything we do?"

"Yes," said the Queen.

"Is Elf in it?"

"Yes," said the Queen.

"Is Lord Buzzle in it, too?" asked Twig.

"Yes," said the Queen.

"And—the Sparrows?" asked Twig.

"Yes," said the Queen.

"And—Old Boy, the ice-wagon horse?" asked Twig. "And—and—Old Girl, the cat?"

"Yes—yes," said the Queen.

"Well, how did we all *get* in it?" asked Twig.

"By magic," said the Queen.

"Magic!" said Twig. "Who *did* the magic? Elf, I suppose!"

The Queen didn't answer. She only smiled. Then she asked, "What happened before Elf came?"

"Before Elf came?" said Twig. "Why—nothing!"

"Weren't you expecting a pretty little fairy before Elf came?" asked the Queen.

"Yes, Your Majesty," said Twig. And then she said, "Oh! You mean—expecting a fairy was *the beginning?*"

"Yes," said the Queen.

"You mean—expecting a fairy was *the magic?*" asked Twig.

"Yes," said the Queen.

"I didn't *know* I was doing magic," said Twig.

"Of course you didn't," said the Queen, smiling and taking one more little stitch. "You never know. That's the beauty of it."

"You mean, the beauty of my—my—" asked Twig, "my—"

"I-ma-gi-na-tion," said the Queen, very slowly and patiently, smoothing the elbow of Lord Buzzle's coat over her knee.

Twig looked toward the other side of the dandelion, where Elf and Lord Buzzle were sitting. She held both her hands over her mouth. Then, right away, she let her hands drop. She sat still as a statue, staring at the elbow of Lord Buzzle's coat, on the Queen's knee. The hole was darned! "Your Majesty—" whispered Twig, "does—going to Fairyland—*have*—to be—the end?"

"Something has to be the end, sometime," said the Queen, breaking off her Cobb-Webb thread and winding it round and round her needle. "But ends are also beginnings, you know. Every single story has a beginning at its end."

"Really? O-o-o-o-o-oh!" said Twig, nodding her head up and down. "I see! You mean—going to Fairyland would be a perfectly lovely *beginning!* The beginning of *another* story!"

"Yes," said the Queen, putting her needle into her little green bag. "That's just what I mean."

Suddenly, Twig slipped from the leaf. She stood on tiptoe. She took a little step on tiptoe. She smiled at the Queen. "Will you pardon me for a minute, please, Your Majesty?" she asked. "I seem to feel like dancing!" She took another little step on tiptoe. She waved her arms very, very gracefully. Then she went dancing round and round the dandelion, fast—fast—as fast as she could go!

129

"Pardon me, Mr. Buzzle, sir," said Elf, "but—see this book?"

Lord Buzzle not only looked at the book through his gold-rimmed spectacles—he reached right out and took it! "Well well well well well well well!" he said. "Where did you pick *this* up, young whipper-snapper?"

"In a corner," said Elf.

"Exactly where I laid it down!" said Lord Buzzle. Then he said, "Do you happen to know who wrote it, young whipper-snapper?"

"Who wrote—the book, you mean, Mr. Buzzle, sir?" said Elf. "Why, no!"

Lord Buzzle looked at Elf through his gold-rimmed spectacles. "Allow me to introduce myself—" he said grandly, "Lord Buzzle Cobb-Webb!"

"Why, Mr. Buzzle, sir!" said Elf. "You mean—*you* wrote it?"

"That's exactly what I mean," said Lord Buzzle.

"How long did it take you, Mr. Buzzle, sir?" asked Elf.

Lord Buzzle closed his eyes and wrinkled up his forehead, as if he were doing a very hard problem. At last he said, "One hour"—and opened his eyes.

"One hour! Is *that* all!" said Elf.

"One hour is all it took to write it," said Lord Buzzle. "But it took fifty-seven years to learn *what* to write!"

"Fifty-seven years!" said Elf. "Whew!"

And a little piece of Lord Buzzle's fluffy white hair came loose from his head and went floating away. He watched it go, through his gold-rimmed spectacles.

"*Sodasodasarsaparilla!*" he whispered.

"I'm sorry, sir!" said Elf.

"Young whipper-snapper!" said Lord Buzzle crossly. Then, quickly, he opened the book he had written and turned to page thirty-seven. "Now, this page . . . here . . ." he said, tapping one of his fingers up and down on it.

Elf climbed up beside him to look. "Say!" said Elf. "That's the page I used on Twig!"

"Used on Twig?" asked Lord Buzzle. "What do you mean by that, young whipper-snapper?"

"Well, Mr. Buzzle, sir," explained Elf, "Twig wasn't always like this, you know. Twig was"—Elf leaned away over close to Lord Buzzle and whispered into his ear—"ten times as big as the house! She really was, Mr. Buzzle, sir!"

"Well well well well well well well!" said Lord Buzzle. "So you made her what she is now, did you, young whipper-snapper?"

"Yes, sir," said Elf proudly.

"And how in the sodasoda—er . . . how did you do it?"

"By magic, sir," said Elf.

"Magic!" said Lord Buzzle. "Well well well well well well well! So you're interested in magic, are you, young whipper-snapper?"

"I'll say I am, Mr. Buzzle, sir!" squeaked Elf. "I'll *say* I am!" And his whole face shone with saying that he was.

"And do you mean to tell me, young whipper-snapper," said Lord Buzzle, "that you did what you did from this page —here? This page—*here*—young whipper-snapper?"

"Yes, sir," said Elf.

"Well well well well well well well!" said Lord Buzzle. "What else have you done, young whipper-snapper?"

"By magic . . . you mean . . . Mr. Buzzle, sir?" said Elf. "Well, I—er . . . I—er . . . I—er . . . I—er . . . I—well, *I* did it!"

"*Sodasodasarsaparilla!*" whispered Lord Buzzle. "Did what?"

"Started the potatoes to dancing," said Elf, "down in Old Shoemaker's cellar."

"So *you're* the young whipper-snapper who started all that trouble, are you?" said Lord Buzzle, tapping one of his fingers up and down on page thirty-seven. Then he tapped two of his fingers up and down. And after a while he began to tap *three* of his fingers.

"Listen, Mr. Buzzle, sir!" said Elf, giving the little old gentleman's shirt sleeve a tug. "I didn't mean to start trouble! Honestly, Mr. Buzzle, sir! You see, Mr. Buzzle, sir— I didn't have anything to do while I was sitting on the sack of potatoes, down in Old Shoemaker's cellar, waiting for the story to begin again. I didn't have anything to do but think.

So I used to think about magic. I used to think what fun it

would be if I could make all the potatoes jump out of the sack and go dancing around the cellar, Mr. Buzzle, sir! And then, one day, they just—did it!

"Out jumped all the potatoes—and around the cellar they went, dancing! And it *was* fun, sir! It surely was fun! But when it came almost time for the story to begin again, I tried to stop them, and—well, sir, I couldn't! So I thought I'd better go and tell Old Shoemaker to stop them. Up the steps I ran, *three* at a time, sir! And there was Old Shoemaker, in the kitchen. But he wouldn't listen. He just said '*Sh!*' and went on talking to his Wife. So I thought I'd better go and find out how to stop the potatoes, myself. Out of the kitchen I ran, sir! And there I was, right in the Public Lib'ary! A lot of books were there. But the books were all too big for me! Well, finally I found *this* book, sir, over in a corner. So I sat down in the corner and opened it and tried to find out how to stop the potatoes. I tried and tried, sir, and I've been trying ever since, but—"

"Well well well well well well well!" said Lord Buzzle. "What seems to be the trouble? Can't you *read* it?"

"Well, Mr. Buzzle, sir," explained Elf, "I—er . . . I—er . . . I—er . . . I—er . . . well—no, sir, I can't."

Lord Buzzle leaned away over close to Elf and whispered into his ear, "*Neither can I!*"

A great magician who couldn't even read his own book! "Whew!" said Elf.

And a little piece of Lord Buzzle's fluffy white hair came loose from his head and went floating away. He watched it go, through his gold-rimmed spectacles.

"Now listen to me, young whipper-snapper!" he said.

"I'm sorry, sir!" said Elf.

"Listen to me!" said Lord Buzzle.

"I won't ever do it again, sir!" said Elf. "I promise I won't ever do it again, Mr. B-b-b—"

"Listen to me!" said Lord Buzzle once more.

"I'm listening," said Elf.

"For a long time," said Lord Buzzle, tapping four of his fingers up and down on page thirty-seven, "I've been looking for a young whipper-snapper who could someday go on doing what I have done, go on being what I have been, take my name and step right into my shoes. And here, at last, I have found just such a young whipper-snapper!" Lord Buzzle looked straight at Elf, through his gold-rimmed spectacles, and *smiled.*

"You mean—me?" said Elf, very much surprised. *"Me!* Step into *your* shoes!"

"You're just the one I mean," said Lord Buzzle. "And what's the matter with my shoes?"

"Well, Mr. Buzzle, sir," said Elf, reaching out his foot and putting it beside one of Lord Buzzle's, "they're rather *big!*"

"The bigger the better!" said Lord Buzzle, looking down at them through his gold-rimmed spectacles. Then he said, "Young whipper-snapper—how would you like to go back to Fairyland with me and be my helper?"

"Go—to *Fairyland!* . . . With—*you,* Mr. Buzzle, sir? . . . And—be your *helper?* . . . How would I *like* to!" squeaked Elf. "Say! Do you *really mean it?*"

Lord Buzzle winked at Elf through his gold-rimmed spectacles. Of course he really meant it! "And if you work hard—if you're not lazy, like the young whipper-snapper who *was* my helper," he added, "you'll be a great magician yourself in fifty-seven years."

A great magician himself! In fifty-seven years! Elf had to hold both his hands over his mouth to keep from saying "Whew!" Then he let his hands drop. He looked down at his potato-skin clothes. "I'm afraid I can't ever be a great magician, sir," he said sadly.

"Why are you afraid you can't?" asked Lord Buzzle.

"Well, Mr. Buzzle, sir," said Elf, "who's going to sit on the sack of potatoes, down in Old Shoemaker's cellar?"

"The lazy young whipper-snapper who *was* my helper,"

said Lord Buzzle, "is sitting down in Old Shoemaker's cellar this very minute. And I shouldn't be surprised if the story had begun again several times already! So there's nothing to worry about now, is there?"

"Well, Mr. Buzzle, sir," said Elf, *"now*—I'll have to ask Twig! . . . Whew!"

And, before a little piece of Lord Buzzle's fluffy white hair could come loose from his head and float away, Elf had slipped from the leaf and was running around the dandelion, as fast as he could go.

★

Sparrow, hopping around and around the Kerchief. "WHAT IN THE NAME OF COMMON SENSE IS THIS?"

"That's called the Royal Magical Cobb-Webb Kerchief, after Lord Buzzle," explained Twig. "We're all going to Fairyland on it in just a minute!"

And, sure enough, in just a minute Lord Buzzle said, "Well well well well well well well! Is everybody ready?"

"Yippee!" squeaked Elf, jumping onto the Kerchief. " 'Bye, Mrs. Sparrow! 'Bye, Sparrow!"

" 'Bye, little fellow—LITTLE SPORT!" said the Sparrows.

"Good-bye, Mrs. Sparrow!" said the Queen, smiling very sweetly. "I've had a lovely time."

" 'Bye, ma'am!" said Mrs. Sparrow, making a curtsy as best she could. "Come again! We'd love to have you!"

"Thank you!" said the Queen politely. "I'd love to come! . . . Good-bye, Sparrow!" And she stepped onto the Kerchief.

"SO YOU'RE LEAVING US, QUEENIE!" shouted Sparrow. "WELL, IT'S BEEN A PLEASURE! . . . SO LONG, CAPTAIN!"

"Good-bye, sir!" said Mrs. Sparrow.

Lord Buzzle made a low bow. "Good-bye, good-bye!" he said, looking from Sparrow to Mrs. Sparrow through his gold-rimmed spectacles. Then he put on his high hat, stepped onto the Kerchief with the help of Elf, and sat down beside the Queen.

"Oh, Mrs. Sparrow!" said Twig, putting her arms round her as far as they would go. "I hate to say good-bye!"

"Oh, little missy!" said Mrs. Sparrow. "So do I! It surely will be lonesome here without you!"

" 'Bye, Sparrow!" said Twig, with her arms still around Mrs. Sparrow.

"SO LONG, TWIGGIE!" shouted Sparrow.

Twig took her arms from around Mrs. Sparrow. Then she stepped onto the Kerchief and sat down beside Elf.

And just then there was a loud *Squa-a-a-w-w-w-k!* from the Sparrows' nest. "Oh! Mrs. Sparrow! Say good-bye to the children for me, will you?" squeaked Twig.

"Me too!" squeaked Elf.

"All right, little missy—little fellow," said Mrs. Sparrow.

Then Lord Buzzle raised his arms and began waving them in the air. Elf raised *his* arms, to help.

"Up you go!" chirped Mrs. Sparrow.

"Oh, wait a minute, please, Mr. Buzzle, sir!" said Elf.

So Lord Buzzle waited, with his arms in the air, while Elf ran across to the dandelion, and back again with the little red book.

"Whew!" said Elf, sitting down beside Twig once more. "We almost forgot it!"

And a little piece of Lord Buzzle's fluffy white hair came loose from his head and went floating away. He watched it go, through his gold-rimmed spectacles.

"*Sodasodasarsaparilla!*" he whispered.

"I'm sorry, sir!" said Elf.

"Young whipper-snapper!" said Lord Buzzle crossly. Then he began waving his arms again.

Again Mrs. Sparrow chirped, "Up you go!"

But this time it was Twig who said, "Oh, wait a minute, please, Mr. Buzzle, sir!"

So Lord Buzzle waited again.

Twig took a deep breath and thought what to say. She took another deep breath and thought what to say. She took three deep breaths and thought what to say three times. Then, at last, she said, "Your Majesty—I'm not going." She

took a fourth deep breath. "I'm just a plain, ordinary little girl, Your Majesty," she said. "Oh! quite a big one, really —not like this. Elf made me like this, by magic. But I can't keep on being like this. . . . You see," she said, "I have a Mama and a Papa—the same as Mrs. Sparrow's children have her and Sparrow. Mrs. Sparrow's children need to stay with her and Sparrow, till they're grown up anyway—the same as I need to stay with my Mama and my Papa till I'm grown up. . . . But it's not so much that I need to stay—it's really that . . . it's really that . . . it's really that . . . well, I guess it's really that I *want* to stay! . . . Do you understand, Your Majesty?"

The Queen smiled and reached over and patted Twig's cheek, very, very gently. Of course she understood!

" 'Bye, Elf!" whispered Twig.

" 'Bye, Twig!" whispered Elf.

Slowly Twig crawled off the Kerchief. She sat down on the ground and doubled up her legs and covered her face with her hands.

Quietly Lord Buzzle waved his arms. Quietly Elf waved his. Quietly the Royal Magical Cobb-Webb Kerchief rose from the ground and went floating up . . . up . . . up out of the back yard . . . up into the sky . . . up over the city . . . and away.

Quietly Mrs. Sparrow cocked her head and said, "Poor Twiggie! Poor little missy!" Then she spread her wings and flew up to the nest.

Even Sparrow was quiet, for once. He hopped to the stream and took a drink of drainpipe water. Then he, too, spread his wings and flew up to the nest.

"Twig! . . . *Twig!*" A voice was calling. It was her Mama's voice.

Quickly Twig took her hands from her face. She jumped up. She looked down at her feet. My, but her feet were BIG! . . . She looked down at the little house. Why, it was hardly any higher than her feet! . . . She looked all around.

"Well, did you ever!" she said, with her hands on her hips.

She was changed back.

★

UP THE STEPS

TWIG WAS GOING UP the steps, from the back yard. They were zigzag steps and there were a good many of them. Halfway up the first flight of steps she stopped and turned and looked down. Then, very slowly, she went climbing up again.

At the top of the first flight of steps was the back porch which belonged to the first floor. And there sat old Mr. Cobb, the landlord, reading the newspaper, as usual.

"How-do, Mr. Cobb, sir!" said Twig, as politely as she could, because he was the landlord. "How's the world?"

"Discombobulated!" said Mr. Cobb, folding up his newspaper. "Dis-com-bob-u-la-ted!" he said again, very slowly

146

and patiently, shaking his head and tucking the newspaper under his chair.

Twig was glad he had thought of his word, at last. She turned to go. Then she turned back. Mr. Cobb was reaching into his pocket for something. Maybe he was going to do some magic! So Twig waited. And pretty soon Mr. Cobb took out a stick of gum. He laid it on the palm of his hand, turned his hand over, and when he turned it up again, the stick of gum was gone!

Quickly, Twig slipped her hand into *her* pocket. And there it was!

Mr. Cobb winked at her, through his gold-rimmed spectacles.

"Oh! Thanks, Mr. Cobb, sir!" said Twig. Then she waved good-bye and went skipping up the next flight of steps.

At the top of the next flight of steps was the back porch which belonged to the second floor. And there stood Blondie Buzzle taking down the wash which she had been hanging up, before.

"Hello, Twig!" said Blondie, with a clothespin in her mouth.

"Hel-lo!" said Twig, smiling very sweetly because Blondie looked so beautiful. She had her very best long pink dress on, and her smart little fluffy brown fur.

"Guess what!" said Blondie, taking the clothespin out of her mouth.

So Twig guessed. "What?"

"We're expecting my sister's little fellow tomorrow," said Blondie. "You know—the one who was here before?"

"The one who's interested in magic?" asked Twig.

148

"Yes," said Blondie. "And we're going to the park. Mr. Cobb is going, too. How would you like to go with us?"

"Go—*with you!* . . . To the—*park!* . . . How would I—*like to* . . . *Oh!* Your—" Twig held both her hands over her mouth for a minute. Why, she had almost called Blondie Your Majesty! Why, this was just like being in the story! "Oh! *Blondie!*" said Twig. "Do you *really mean it?*"

Blondie smiled. Of course she really meant it!

"Thanks, Blondie!" said Twig. "I'd like to very much!" Then she waved good-bye and went skipping up the *next* flight of steps.

At the top of the *next* flight of steps was the back porch which belonged to the third floor. And there sat Mrs. Webb, on the big broken box, holding her little baldheaded baby.

"Hello, little missy!" said Mrs. Webb. "I wonder if you'd mind holding the baby for a minute, while I go into the house. I thought I heard Webb come in!"

"Oh, I wouldn't mind a bit!" said Twig.

"Sit right down here then," said Mrs. Webb, getting up.

So Twig sat down on the big broken box and took Mrs. Webb's baby in her arms, while Mrs. Webb went into the house. *"Dear!"* whispered Twig, leaning away down close and kissing the baby very, very softly, on the top of his little bald head.

Mrs. Webb came right out. "It wasn't Webb at all!"
she said. "T-t-t-t! I wonder where he can be?" She took
the baby back in *her* arms. And Twig jumped up.

"Mrs. Webb—" she said, turning her toes in and out,
in and out, "could I—could I—could I take care of your
baby *again*—sometime?"

Mrs. Webb began to chuckle. She just couldn't help it.
She chuckled till her whole dress shook. "Why, of course,
little missy!" she said. "Any time you like!"

"Oh! Thanks, Mrs. Webb!" said Twig. Then she went
skipping up the last flight of steps.

At the top of the last flight of steps was the back porch
which belonged to the fourth floor. And that was where
Twig lived, with her Mama and her Papa.

150

Her Papa had just finished taking his snooze. He was sitting on the edge of the old, old sofa folding up his handkerchief.

"Oh-ho-ho-ho-hmmmmm!" he yawned. Then he said, "Well, if it isn't Twiggie! Where in the world have you been?"

"In the back yard," said Twig, without mentioning the story, because her Papa might think it was silly.

"Well, well!" said her Papa, putting his handkerchief into his pocket. "Your Mama and I were beginning to think you'd gone away for good!" He yawned again. Then he got up from the old, old sofa and went into the house.

"Who's that?" asked Twig's Mama, inside.

"Just Twig," said her Papa, yawning once more. "Oh-ho-ho-ho-hmmm!—just Twig."

Twig reached into her pocket and took out Mr. Cobb's stick of gum. She stepped to the porch's wooden railing and stood leaning against it, unwrapping the piece of shiny paper and looking down into the back yard.

My, but the back yard was far away now! It was so far away that the little house seemed no higher than a thimble; the stream no wider than a piece of grocery string; the dandelion no larger than a bright green spot, down there on the bare brown ground.

Twig thought about all that had happened in her little world today. She thought about tomorrow, and all that would happen then: expecting Blondie's sister's little fellow—taking care of Mrs. Webb's baby—going to the park —and everything that *might* happen, by magic!

Oh! Wasn't this lovely? Wasn't *this* a perfectly lovely end? It was like waiting for the story to begin all over again! And it was a little like something else, too. It was a little like making a wish, and having the wish come true.

Twig let go of the piece of shiny paper and watched while it floated down—down—down. Then she took a bite of the stick of gum and looked up into the sky.

She looked and looked. And pretty soon she saw a little tiny star, no bigger than a toothpaste top, come out right above the back yard. She saw it come out and begin to twinkle, all by itself. Why! It wasn't evening yet. There weren't any other stars around. There was nothing around except plain, ordinary sky. But the little star kept twinkling. And—somehow—the sky didn't seem so plain and ordinary any more. Why! Even a little star no bigger than a toothpaste top made quite a difference—a little star, twinkling all by itself, made a difference in the whole sky!

★

Mr. Pine's Purple House
story and pictures by Leonard Kessler

Mr. Pine lives on Vine Street in a little white house, in one of FIFTY white houses all in a line. How can he tell which one is his? Find out how Mr. Pine solves this problem in his own special way.

Mr. Pine's Mixed-up Signs
story and pictures by Leonard Kessler

Mr. Pine paints all new signs for Little Town, but loses his glasses. Pure chaos results when he puts the signs up anyway! Who took his glasses and how does Mr. Pine solve the problem of all those mixed-up signs?

Miss Twiggley's Tree
written and illustrated by Dorothea Warren Fox

Why did Miss Twiggley live in a tree? Why did she send her dog, Puss, out to do the shopping? Why does she always run away and hide when people come to visit? The townspeople think this is all simply disgraceful, but they come to appreciate Miss Twiggley when a hurricane hits town.

Miss Suzy
by Miriam Young, illustrated by Arnold Lobel

Miss Suzy is a little gray squirrel who lives happily in her oak-tree home until she is chased away by some mean red squirrels. But soon she finds a beautiful dollhouse and meets a band of brave toy soldiers. How they help each other creates a gentle, old-fashioned tale that has captured the imaginations of both girls and boys alike for over forty years.

The Brother's Lionheart
by Astrid Lindgren, illustrated by Ilon Wikland
Jonathan and Karl Lionheart share many exciting adventures after their death when they are reunited in Nangiyala, the land from which sagas come. Also back in print is *Mio, My Son* by Lindgren.

The Mad Scientists' Club series
by Bertrand Brinley, illustrated by Charles Geer
A strange sea monster appears on Strawberry Lake… a fortune is unearthed from an old cannon…and a valuable dinosaur egg is stolen. These are among the twelve short stories contained in first two Mad Scientists' Club books. The third volume *The Big Kerplop!* is a full-length novel in which Henry Mulligan and the gang track a mysterious object that the Air Force has accidentally plunged into Strawberry Lake. The fourth book, a previously unpublished novel, is on the way!

Big Susan
written and illustrated by Elizabeth Orton Jones
The Doll family awaits the one wonderful night of Christmas Eve, when all dolls come alive, when they will be able to speak and move without help from Susan. They prove to themselves there is more to Christmas than just presents, and that miracles can happen anywhere — even in a dollhouse.

Purple House Press is dedicated to reviving many wonderful books from your childhood. We've brought back more than twenty great titles in just four short years. Please check our website for news on our latest releases!

www.PurpleHousePress.com